THE FARMINGTON COMMUNITY LIBRARY
FARMINGTON HILLS BRANCH
32737 WEST TWELVE MILE ROAD
FARMINGTON HILLS, MI 48334-3302
(248) 553-0300

W9-DET-086

JUL 22 2011

JUL 2 2 2011

Alice-Miranda

at School

Alice-Miranda

30036010945259

at School

JACQUELINE HARVEY

DELACORTE PRESS

This is a work of fiction. Names, characters, places, and incidents
either are the product of the author's imagination or are used fictitiously. Any resemblance to
actual persons, living or dead, events, or locales is entirely coincidental.

Text copyright © 2010 by Jacqueline Harvey
Jacket and interior illustrations copyright © 2010 by J. Yi

All rights reserved. Published in the United States by Delacorte Press, an imprint of
Random House Children's Books, a division of Random House, Inc., New York.
Originally published in paperback by
Random House Australia, Sydney, in 2010.

Delacorte Press is a registered trademark and the colophon is a
trademark of Random House, Inc.

Visit us on the Web! www.randomhouse.com/kids

Educators and librarians, for a variety of teaching tools, visit us at
www.randomhouse.com/teachers

Library of Congress Cataloging-in-Publication Data
Harvey, Jacqueline.
Alice-Miranda at school / Jacqueline Harvey. — 1st American ed.
p. cm.
Summary: Soon after arriving at the Winchesterfield-Downsfordvale Academy for Proper Young
Ladies, resourceful seven-and-one-quarter-year-old Alice-Miranda finds her new boarding school
to be a very curious establishment with no flowers in the gardens, a headmistress that has not
been seen for years, and a mysterious stranger that seems to be hiding out on the premises.
ISBN 978-0-385-73993-1 (hc : alk. paper) — ISBN 978-0-375-89858-7 (ebook) —
ISBN 978-0-385-90811-5 (glb : alk. paper)
[1. Boarding schools—Fiction. 2. Schools—Fiction. 3. Secrets—Fiction.
4. Mystery and detective stories.] I. Title.
PZ7.H2674785Al 2011
[Fic]—dc22
2010023723

The text of this book is set in 12-point Century Schoolbook.

Book design by Marci Senders

Printed in the United States of America

10 9 8 7 6 5 4 3 2

First American Edition

Random House Children's Books supports the First Amendment
and celebrates the right to read.

For Sandy Campbell,
a dear friend much loved and missed

And for my husband, Ian—
who reads and listens and laughs (a lot)

Chapter 1

Alice-Miranda Highton-Smith-Kennington-Jones waved goodbye to her parents at the gate.

"Goodbye, Mummy. Please try to be brave." Her mother sobbed loudly in reply. "Enjoy your golf, Daddy. I'll see you at the end of term." Her father sniffled into his handkerchief.

Before they had time to wave her goodbye, Alice-Miranda skipped back down the hedge-lined path into her new home.

Winchesterfield-Downsfordvale Academy for Proper Young Ladies had a tradition dating back two and a half centuries. Alice-Miranda's mother, aunt, grandmother, great-grandmother and so on had all gone there. But none had been so young or so willing.

It had come as quite a shock to Alice-Miranda's parents to learn that she had telephoned the school to see if she could start early—she was, after all, only seven and one-quarter years old, and not due to start for another year. But after two years at her current school, Ellery Prep, she felt ready for bigger things. Besides, Alice-Miranda had always been different from other children. She loved her parents dearly and they loved her, but boarding school appealed to her sense of adventure.

"It's much better this way," Alice-Miranda had said with a smile. "You both work so hard and you have far more important things to do than run after me. This way I can do all my activities at school. Imagine, Mummy—no more waiting around while I'm at ballet or piano or riding lessons."

"But darling, I don't mind a bit," her mother protested.

"I know you don't," Alice-Miranda had agreed, "but you should think about my being away as a holiday. And then at the end there's all the excitement of coming home, except that it's me coming home to you." She'd hugged her mother and stroked her father's brow as she handed them a gigantic box of tissues.

Although they didn't want her to go, they knew there was no point arguing. Once Alice-Miranda made up her mind there was no turning back.

Her teacher, Miss Critchley, hadn't seemed the least surprised by Alice-Miranda's plans.

"Of course, we'll all miss her terribly," Miss Critchley had explained to Alice-Miranda's parents. "But that daughter of yours is more than up to it. I can't imagine there's any reason to stop her."

And so Alice-Miranda went.

Winchesterfield-Downsfordvale sat upon three thousand emerald-colored acres. A tapestry of Georgian buildings dotted the campus, with Winchesterfield Manor the jewel in the crown. Along its labyrinth of corridors hung huge portraits of past headmistresses with serious stares and old-fashioned clothes. The trophy cabinets glittered with treasure and the foyer was lined with priceless antiques. There was not a thing out of place. But from the moment Alice-Miranda entered the grounds she had a strange feeling that something was missing—and she was usually right about her strange feelings.

The headmistress, Miss Grimm, had not come out of her study to meet her. The school's secretary, Miss Higgins, had met Alice-Miranda and her parents at the gate, looking rather surprised to see them.

"I'm terribly sorry, Mr. and Mrs. Highton-Smith-Kennington-Jones. There must have been a mix-up with the dates—Alice-Miranda is a day early," Miss Higgins had explained.

Her parents had said that it was no bother and they would come back again tomorrow. But Miss Higgins was appalled at the idea of causing such inconvenience and offered to take care of Alice-Miranda until the house mistress arrived.

It was Miss Higgins who had interviewed Alice-Miranda some weeks ago, when Alice-Miranda had first contacted the school. At that meeting, Alice-Miranda had thought Miss Higgins quite lovely, with her kindly eyes and pretty smile. But today she couldn't help noticing that Miss Higgins seemed a little flustered and talked as though she were in a race.

Miss Higgins showed Alice-Miranda to her room and suggested she take a stroll around the school. "I'll come and find you and take you to see Cook about some lunch in a little while."

Alice-Miranda unpacked her case, folded her clothes and put them neatly away into one of the tall chests of drawers. The room contained two single beds on opposite walls, matching chests and bedside tables. In a tidy alcove, two timber desks, each with a black swivel chair, stood side by side. The furniture was what her mother might have called functional. Not beautiful, but all very useful. The room's only hint of elegance came from the fourteen-foot ceiling with ornate cornices and the polished timber floor.

Alice-Miranda was delighted to find an envelope addressed to *Miss Alice-Miranda Highton-Smith-Kennington-Jones* propped against her pillow.

"How lovely—my own special letter," Alice-Miranda said out loud. She looked at the slightly tatty brown bear in her open suitcase. "Isn't that sweet, Brummel?"

She slid her finger under the opening and pulled out a very grand-looking note on official school paper. It read:

WINCHESTERFIELD-DOWNSFORDVALE ACADEMY FOR PROPER YOUNG LADIES

Dear Miss Highton-Smith-Kennington-Jones,

Welcome to Winchesterfield-Downsfordvale Academy for Proper Young Ladies. It is expected that you will work extremely hard at all times and strive to achieve your very best. You must obey without question all of the school rules, of which there is a copy attached to this letter. Furthermore, you must ensure that your behavior is such that it always brings credit to you, your family and this establishment.

Yours sincerely,
Miss Ophelia Grimm
Headmistress

WINCHESTERFIELD-DOWNSFORDVALE ACADEMY FOR PROPER YOUNG LADIES SCHOOL RULES

1. Hair ribbons in regulation colors and a width of 3/4 of an inch will be tied with double overhand bows.
2. Shoes will be polished twice a day with boot polish and brushes.
3. Shoelaces will be washed each week by hand.
4. Head lice are banned.

5. All times tables to 20 must be learned by heart by the age of 9.
6. Bareback horse riding is not permitted in the quadrangle.
7. All girls will learn to play golf, croquet and bridge.
8. Licorice will not be consumed after 5 p.m.
9. Unless invited by the headmistress, parents will not enter school buildings.
10. Homesickness will not be tolerated.

Alice-Miranda put the letter down and cuddled the little bear. "Oh, Brummel, I can't wait to meet Miss Grimm—she sounds like she's very interested in her students."

Alice-Miranda folded the letter and placed it in the top drawer. She would memorize the school rules later. She popped her favorite photos of Mummy and Daddy on her bedside table and positioned the bear carefully on her bed.

"You be a brave boy, Brummel." She ruffled his furry head. "I'm off to explore, and when I get back I'll tell you all about it."

Chapter 2

Alice-Miranda discovered lots of things. There was an enormous library, a swimming pool and a lake, fields to play games on, tennis courts, stables and classrooms, which—if she stood on tippy-toes and peered through the windows—looked to have the very best equipment. Winchesterfield-Downsfordvale had everything a school could possibly want and more, but she still couldn't help feeling that something wasn't right. There was something missing, something important that should have been there but wasn't.

Alice-Miranda thought and thought, but she couldn't work it out.

She was walking past the kitchen when she heard the unmistakable sound of muffled sobbing. She opened the screen door and marched straight inside. There among the pots and pans, amid a maze of stainless steel, sat Cook. The words on her lips bubbled and frothed like the pot on the stove behind her.

"She never likes anything I make. All that perfectly good food going to waste. I might as well be invisible." Cook blew her nose into a tatty tissue, then wiped the back of her hand across her apron.

Alice-Miranda walked right up and tapped the woman on the shoulder. In one movement Cook seized the rolling pin in front of her and leapt to her feet.

"Hello, Cook—" Alice-Miranda stopped and inhaled deeply. "Ohh!" she exclaimed. "May I try one of those delicious-looking brownies there on the bench? The smell is driving my stomach mad."

Cook didn't know what to say. Children didn't enter her kitchen, let alone ask for something to eat. She hesitated, slowly lowered the rolling pin back onto the bench and gave a funny sort of half-nod.

Alice-Miranda picked up the nearest brownie and took a giant bite. She was careful not to drop any crumbs.

"That's the yummiest brownie I have ever tasted.

And you know, I have had some rather good ones. Last summer Mummy and Daddy took me to Switzerland and we had lunch with their funny old friend the baron and his cook baked me some brownies but they weren't anything to compare with this one. You must simply be the most superb brownie cook in the whole wide world."

Cook couldn't think of a thing to say. It was probably best, given that her usual response was to growl at anyone who dared to comment on her cooking.

Alice-Miranda held out her hand (she wiped the crumbs delicately on her handkerchief and popped it into her pocket first). "Please excuse me for being so rude. My name is Alice-Miranda Highton-Smith-Kennington-Jones and I am very pleased to meet you, Mrs. . . . ?"

Cook frowned and somewhat reluctantly took Alice-Miranda's tiny hand in hers.

"Smith," Cook replied with a puzzled look.

"Well, Mrs. Smith, I am so pleased to have met you. I can't wait to eat your delicious meals, and I want to say thank you very much for the brownie. You know"—Alice-Miranda tilted her head and thought for a moment—"we might even be related somehow. My mother was a Highton-Smith, and before that someone must have been simply a Smith."

Cook shook some imaginary crumbs from her apron and hesitantly asked Alice-Miranda if she would like a glass of milk to have with the rest of her brownie.

"Oh yes, please. Now, Mrs. Smith, I have a question. I've been looking all around this wonderful school, which has everything I could possibly imagine a school would ever need and more, but there's something missing and I can't work out what it is." Alice-Miranda bit her lip as she pondered the problem.

Mrs. Smith couldn't think of anything either. She believed it was just about the poshest school in the world. So after they had thought for a while, they ate their brownies and drank their milk and Mrs. Smith told Alice-Miranda about her grandchildren who lived all the way over the sea in the United States of America. Alice-Miranda thought that was marvelous and asked if she had been to visit them and see the Grand Canyon and the Empire State Building and all the other amazing things America has to offer.

Mrs. Smith shook her head and whispered sadly that she hadn't ever been.

"Why not?" Alice-Miranda asked.

"Well, there'd be no one to cook Miss Grimm's dinners, then, would there?" Mrs. Smith mumbled.

"I'm sure we could find someone to step in, just for a little while," said Alice-Miranda.

Mrs. Smith fiddled with the pocket on the front of her apron. "I did ask once, a long time ago, and I was told that if I needed to take a holiday, then I should make it a permanent one." Her voice quavered as she spoke.

"That's terrible." Alice-Miranda shook her head. "I'll speak with Miss Grimm right away." She stood up and headed for the door, but after a moment she turned back and faced Cook. "Mrs. Smith, holidays are very important. Everyone needs to have one sometime or another. I think Miss Grimm's being a little bit selfish."

Mrs. Smith stood with her mouth open as this tiny girl with cascading chocolate curls marched off into the garden. She felt a tickle around her mouth and realized that she was doing something she hadn't done in years. She was smiling.

Chapter 3

On her way to see Miss Grimm, Alice-Miranda passed by a large greenhouse. From inside, she heard the sound of shattering glass and a man's angry voice.

"Oh, blast it all!" he bellowed.

Alice-Miranda walked straight to the greenhouse door and pushed it open. A giant of a man stood in front of a workbench, muttering to himself and shaking his fist. There was a little pile of glass on the floor at his feet.

"Good morning, sir," she said, and took herself inside. "My name is Alice-Miranda Highton-Smith-Kennington-Jones and I've just arrived this morning."

The man looked at Alice-Miranda in surprise, but said nothing.

Suddenly Alice-Miranda rushed to the far corner of the greenhouse. "That's the most beautiful *Cypripedium parviflorum* I have ever seen. Last year Mummy and Daddy took me to India and we stayed with Prince Shivaji and he had a beautiful greenhouse with loads of orchids—but there was nothing to compare with this lady's slipper orchid of yours. It's truly amazing. You must be the best gardener in the whole world, Mr. . . ."

Alice-Miranda walked back toward him and held out her hand.

He took her tiny fingers into his large paw and gulped. "Charlie," he whispered hoarsely. "The girls call me Charlie."

"Well, that won't do at all." Alice-Miranda shook her head. "I will call you Mr. Charles. Anyone who grows such extraordinary flowers deserves more respect. Now, Mr. Charles, I see that you have a kettle on that little stove in the corner. Shall I make you a cup of tea and then you can tell me what it is that upset you so?"

Charlie nodded slowly. He picked up a dustpan and broom from the back of the bench and began to sweep up the glass at his feet.

Alice-Miranda quickly found some tea for the pot, boiled the kettle and made him the most delicious cup of tea he'd had in ages.

"Now, Mr. Charles, I know that it's most annoying when you break something, but surely that's not why you're so dreadfully cross?" Alice-Miranda smiled kindly.

Charlie looked up. He wasn't a very old man, but years of working outdoors had rewarded him with deep lines running the length of his cheeks. His eyes, the color of cornflowers, seemed to have lost their sparkle.

He began quietly. "Well, miss, it's the flowers. I want to plant flowers, and Miss Grimm, she don't like flowers. The place just looks sad without them." Charlie stared down into his cup. "My dear old dad would turn in his grave knowing the state of this place."

He could hardly believe that this slip of a girl had come along and made him tea, let alone that he was telling her his problems.

"Why would your father be upset?" asked Alice-Miranda.

"He was the gardener here for nigh on forty years before me. It looked a lot different back then, I can tell you."

Alice-Miranda thought for a moment. "Surely it must only be *some* flowers," she decided. "Take, for example, dahlias. My mummy doesn't like them at all. By themselves they're quite lovely, but when they're planted en masse she says that they look like a reef of sea anemones—much better left in the ocean than in the garden."

"I think it's all flowers Miss Grimm hates," Charlie replied.

Alice-Miranda sipped her tea. "You know, I think she must be allergic. That's got to be it. And surely it's impossible to be allergic to *all* flowers."

Alice-Miranda leapt up and placed her teacup in the sink. She had decided to tell Miss Grimm about poor Mr. Charles and his flowers at once. After all, she thought, flowers were one of the joys of life—everyone needed flowers, and surely there were loads of blooms that wouldn't offend her sinuses. Alice-Miranda turned and hesitated at the door.

"Mr. Charles, Winchesterfield-Downsfordvale seems wonderful, but I can't help feeling that there's something missing. I just can't work it out. Do you know what it is?"

Charlie shook his head. "Can't think of a thing, lass. This school has everything and more."

Alice-Miranda said goodbye to Charlie and skipped

through the greenhouse door. As she left, he felt a tingling on his tongue and a tickle on his lips. His face crumpled and his mouth suddenly turned upward. For the first time in years he found himself laughing.

Chapter 4

Passing by the gymnasium, Alice-Miranda heard a piercing scream. She ran toward the open door and saw a young girl, about eleven years of age, sitting on the floor and squealing with the might of ten elephants.

"Hello." Alice-Miranda sat down beside the girl. "My name is Alice-Miranda Highton-Smith-Kennington-Jones and I've just come today."

"Who cares?" the girl spat. "Leave me alone!"

"But you're upset." Alice-Miranda reached out and patted the girl gently on the arm.

"Don't touch me!" the girl yelled, and started screaming again at the top of her lungs.

Alice-Miranda blocked her ears. "I wish you wouldn't do that. It's ever so loud."

Then the girl did the most extraordinary thing. She jumped up and ran down the gym mats, tumbling and twirling.

"My goodness!" exclaimed Alice-Miranda. "You're the best tumbler I have ever seen. Mummy and Daddy once took me to meet a Russian count and we went to a big party and there were tumblers there, but you are much better than they were."

The girl took off again, tumbling backward over and over.

Alice-Miranda clapped and cheered.

The girl stopped. She strode over to where Alice-Miranda was sitting and stood in front of her.

"My name is Jacinta Headlington-Bear and nobody likes me," she declared with her hands firmly on her hips.

"Well, I can't understand why. You are simply the cleverest gymnast," said Alice-Miranda. "Why don't you tell me what's the matter?"

"Miss Grimm won't let me go to the championships. She says that unless I do my homework I can't represent the school."

"That's awfully sad," said Alice-Miranda. "How much homework have you missed?"

"That's just it. It's only one assignment and I was so ill that I was in the infirmary for almost the whole of the term break. I haven't had a holiday at all because my parents were too busy to come and get me. I think it was just an excuse so Mummy could stay in Bordeaux with her friends while Daddy was away on business. I've been trying to catch up, but the championships are on in two weeks and I just can't train and get the stupid project done too."

"What's your assignment about?" Alice-Miranda asked.

"The endangered African elephant," Jacinta replied, pouting. "What would I know about silly old elephants?"

"I can help you," Alice-Miranda offered. "Last year Mummy and Daddy took me on a safari and we got to see the elephants right up close. I have some wonderful photographs."

Jacinta looked as though she'd eaten a bee. None of the other students had ever been so kind to her before—mainly because she was the school's second-best tantrum thrower and the other girls were scared stiff of having to endure a screaming fit like the one Alice-Miranda had just seen.

Alice-Miranda said that she would go at once to talk to Miss Grimm about the homework, and that

Jacinta should meet her at midday and she would help her get it all finished.

Jacinta sat on the mats. She felt a tickly buzz around the corners of her mouth. Anyone who didn't know her would have sworn she almost smiled.

Chapter 5

Alice-Miranda skipped back toward the office, determined to see Miss Grimm immediately. She navigated her way through endless hallways lined with rows and rows of beautiful timber doors. She now had quite a long list of things to talk to Miss Grimm about and would need at least half an hour. When at last she reached the office, she tapped on the door and let herself in. Miss Higgins was seated behind an enormous oak desk. Alice-Miranda could hardly see over the top of it, so she climbed up into the chair opposite to get a better view.

"Hello, Miss Higgins," she said cheerfully.

Miss Higgins recoiled and almost fell off her chair.

"Oh, hello, Alice-Miranda." She sniffled into her handkerchief. "How are you getting on, then?"

"I have had the most wonderful morning and I've met loads of lovely people. I had brownies with Mrs. Smith and a cup of tea with Mr. Charles and the most delightful chat with Jacinta Headlington-Bear and I really would like to tell you all about it. But it doesn't look as though you're having a very good day. Whatever is the matter?" Alice-Miranda leaned forward. "Have you been crying?"

Miss Higgins was so taken aback that she burst into tears.

Alice-Miranda took a clean handkerchief from her pocket and handed it to her.

"Oh, Miss Higgins, you poor thing. Please tell me all about it. Perhaps I can help."

Through tears and sobs Alice-Miranda found out that Miss Higgins was about to get married. She had a lovely fellow from the village, Constable Derby. They had fallen head over heels last summer and on Christmas Eve he had proposed. It was all so wonderful. Except for Miss Grimm.

"She told me that if I marry, I shouldn't bother to come back again. She needs my full devotion and undivided attention and I'm afraid I don't think that's very fair at all."

Alice-Miranda frowned. "Why do you want to stay?"

"It's very complicated, Alice-Miranda, and I wouldn't expect you to understand. You're only a little girl," Miss Higgins replied.

"I know I'm small," said Alice-Miranda, "but I'm quite a good listener." She slid off the leather chair and walked around to Miss Higgins's side of the desk. Alice-Miranda reached up and rested her hand on Miss Higgins's shoulder.

Miss Higgins blew her nose loudly. "It's just, well, I have a very important job to do and I'm afraid that I don't want to leave it up to anyone else."

Alice-Miranda smiled. "Please don't take this the wrong way, Miss Higgins, but I know lots of young ladies who could do this job. My father has twenty girls in his office who could swap places with you in a minute."

Miss Higgins frowned.

Alice-Miranda continued. "I didn't mean to upset you, Miss Higgins. It's just that I thought secretaries did jobs like answering the telephone and writing letters and doing the filing—things like that."

"Yes, I suppose I do all those things, but there are other responsibilities that I *must* look after and, well, I hate to imagine what would happen if I wasn't here," Miss Higgins replied.

Alice-Miranda bit her lip. Her brow furrowed and she seemed lost in her thoughts.

"Miss Higgins, Winchesterfield-Downsfordvale is the most beautiful school in the whole country. The staff are dedicated and the students, I'm sure, are magnificent. But there is something missing from this establishment and it has been nagging me all day."

Miss Higgins dabbed at her eyes and looked up.

"I need to see Miss Grimm immediately," Alice-Miranda continued. "If she doesn't make some changes right away things will only get worse."

"Oh dear. I'm afraid Miss Grimm doesn't see students," Miss Higgins replied quietly.

"I don't understand," said Alice-Miranda. "She's the headmistress. It's her job to see the students and the teachers and all of the people who work in this wonderful school."

"I'm afraid that Miss Grimm doesn't really see anyone. She hasn't seen anyone for, well . . ." Miss Higgins hesitated. "Now, let me think . . . goodness . . . is it really . . . *over ten years now,*" she whispered.

"Ten years! Is she dead?" Alice-Miranda exclaimed loudly.

"No, of course not," Miss Higgins said anxiously. Alice-Miranda couldn't help noticing that her hands were trembling. "She's just very busy."

"But what about assemblies and parent-teacher nights and plays?"

Miss Higgins began shuffling the pile of papers on her desk. "There are the other teachers and, well, nobody seems to fuss. The school just sort of runs itself, and as long as the results are good, I don't see why it matters all that much."

"Then how does she tell people things?" Alice-Miranda frowned.

"She has her ways." Miss Higgins smiled thinly and raised her eyebrows.

Alice-Miranda was not convinced. "Well, that won't do at all." She turned and ran toward the huge double doors that led to the headmistress's study.

"No, Alice-Miranda, you mustn't, you mustn't." Miss Higgins leapt from her chair and rushed to block her path.

Alice-Miranda ducked under Miss Higgins's outstretched arms, grabbed the ancient brass doorknob and pushed open the huge mahogany doors.

Chapter 6

There, in the most enormous chair, sat a tall woman wearing what appeared to be a dressing-gown. Her long blond hair hung limply around her shoulders like an old shawl. Her porcelain face was a blank canvas.

With an elegant fountain pen perched nimbly between her manicured fingers, she was engrossed in the contents of an enormous leather-bound book.

"Hello, Miss Grimm, I am so very pleased to make your acquaintance." Alice-Miranda skipped around to the other side of the desk and held out her tiny hand.

Miss Grimm peered over the top of her very stylish

spectacles. She stared at Alice-Miranda as though she were some kind of nasty stain.

"I'm sorry, Miss Grimm. I couldn't stop her." Miss Higgins stood behind Alice-Miranda, ready to scoop her up and take her away.

"Hello, Miss Grimm, my name is Alice-Miranda Highton-Smith-Kennington-Jones and I have just started here today. Winchesterfield-Downsfordvale is quite the most beautiful school in the world but there are a few things I need to talk to you about most urgently. In fact, I've been worried ever since I arrived that there was something not quite right, and just a few moments ago I think I realized what the matter is. It's most important that we talk right away."

Miss Grimm did not say a word. Alice-Miranda smiled and waited . . . for just a moment.

"I am so sorry. I can see that you are not ready for visitors this morning, so I will go away and come back a little later when you have had time to dress and finish your cup of tea. I have some work to do with Jacinta Headlington-Bear, which I can tell you all about later. What about two p.m.? That's marvelous. Thank you so much for your time, Miss Grimm. It really is a pleasure to meet you and you should be very proud of this beautiful school."

And with that, Alice-Miranda turned on her heel and skipped back from where she came. Miss Higgins rushed after her and hurriedly closed the doors.

Miss Grimm had not said a word during the entire exchange. It appeared that she was completely dumbstruck.

Chapter 7

Alice-Miranda was weary. It had indeed been a very busy morning and she still had to help Jacinta with her homework. She hurried back to her room to give Brummel a full briefing.

Then she used the phone in the common room to call her parents.

"Oh, darling heart, you've changed your mind?" It was fortunate that Alice-Miranda couldn't see the smile on her father's face. "You can be back with us in a blink," he cooed. "I'll send Cyril and Birdy right away."

"Silly Daddy. I'm having a marvelous time. I have met loads of interesting people and it really is the most amazing place. But there are a few things I've noticed and I was wondering if perhaps you could help?"

"Of course, darling—I'll send the builders right away," said her father.

"No, Daddy. I don't need the builders. But I was wondering if perhaps you could spare Mrs. Oliver for a little while."

"Oh, don't tell me the food is awful?" her father moaned.

"Not at all. Cook, whose real name is Mrs. Smith, made the most delicious brownies I have ever tasted. And you know, she might even somehow be related to Mummy's side of the family, seeing as Mummy's a Highton-Smith and I suppose a long time ago someone was just a Smith.

"Anyway, Mrs. Smith has two delicious grandchildren who live all the way over the sea in America and can you believe that she has never been to visit them?"

"That's terrible. Why ever not?" Alice-Miranda's father replied.

"Well, I asked her the same thing and she said that Miss Grimm doesn't let her take holidays because there would be no one to cook her dinners."

"That's a little bit selfish." Her father's voice frowned down the phone line.

"That's exactly what I said. So I was wondering if you could spare Mrs. Oliver, just for a couple of weeks."

"I'll have to check with Mummy, but I think that should be positively wonderful. We're heading off to the town house for some business and I'm sure Dolly would enjoy a change of scenery."

"Oh, thank you, Daddy. You are the best. And please tell Mummy I love her too and I will talk to you both in a little while. And don't worry—Winchesterfield-Downsfordvale is everything I expected and so much more." And with that Alice-Miranda hung up the telephone, hugged Brummel Bear and set off to meet Jacinta.

Chapter 8

At exactly five minutes to two, Alice-Miranda left a smiling Jacinta Headlington-Bear to finish the last sentences of a quite astonishing project on endangered African elephants. She headed back to the office for her meeting with Miss Grimm.

Miss Higgins's door was closed. But propped against it was a letter addressed in beautiful script to *Miss Alice-Miranda Highton-Smith-Kennington-Jones.*

Alice-Miranda loved to receive letters and this was her second of the day. She was surprised anyone had had time to write to her, since she had only left home that morning—but she was pleased nevertheless.

She opened the envelope carefully and pulled the fine notepaper from inside. Her tiny fingers unfolded the sheet. It read:

Miss Alice-Miranda Highton-Smith-
    Kennington-Jones
Winchesterfield-Downsfordvale
    Academy for Proper Young Ladies
Waddlington Lane
Winchesterfield via Downsfordvale

Dear Miss Highton-Smith-Kennington-
    Jones,

Thank you for your interest in
speaking with Miss Grimm today at
two p.m. Unfortunately Miss Grimm is
otherwise engaged and will not be
able to see you today or any other
day. Her time is precious and the
matters of students are not
something with which she cares to
acquaint herself. Please do not
attempt to enter Miss Grimm's study

now or at any other time. The door
is quite firmly locked.

I am your most obedient servant,

Miss Louella Higgins
Personal Secretary to
  the Headmistress
Winchesterfield-Downsfordvale
  Academy for Proper Young Ladies

Alice-Miranda was puzzled. Miss Grimm hadn't objected to the meeting time when she had suggested it. She supposed headmistresses had lots of important things to do, and if Miss Grimm was unavailable, Alice-Miranda would have to try again tomorrow. In the meantime, there were so many people who needed her help that Miss Grimm would just have to wait for now.

Alice-Miranda ran back to the house and called her parents again. This time her mother answered the phone. After a few minutes' conversation, a plan was in place. It seemed that everything was going to work out beautifully for Mrs. Smith after all.

Chapter 9

Alice-Miranda skipped off toward the kitchen. She had to tell Mrs. Smith to pack her things. Mrs. Oliver would be arriving soon and Cook should be ready to head off immediately.

"Hello, Mrs. Smith." Alice-Miranda peered around the kitchen door. Cook was stirring an enormous pot, from which the most mouthwatering smell wafted. Alice-Miranda's nostrils twitched as she tried to work out exactly what was simmering away so temptingly. "My goodness, that smells delicious."

Mrs. Smith turned and smiled at Alice-Miranda— a warm smile that few students had ever seen.

"I've been to see Miss Grimm. I thought we could

have a lovely chat and get you off on a holiday. But she wasn't available and so I haven't spoken to her after all."

"Thank you for trying, miss." A tear welled in the corner of Cook's eye. She brushed it with the back of her hand. "Must be the onions I was chopping." She took a deep breath and pursed her lips together tightly.

"Don't be sad, Mrs. Smith. I've fixed things, and I can just tell Miss Grimm later. I'm sure she won't mind in the least. Mrs. Oliver will be here in a little while, and then Daddy has arranged for you to be picked up and taken to the airport so that you can go on our plane to the United States straight away. The plane has to go over for some special refitting, so it's not the slightest bother at all. But you'll need to pack your suitcase immediately."

Cook's hands were trembling. "But I can't leave without Miss Grimm's approval. I'll lose my job." She looked decidedly pale.

"No, of course you won't. Miss Grimm is only worried that if you're not here there'll be no one to cook her dinners. Isn't that right?" Alice-Miranda asked with a frown.

"Well, that's what I've always been told," Cook replied. "Who's Mrs. Oliver?"

"She's Mummy and Daddy's cook. She can stay for the whole time you're away, and she's really not half bad either," said Alice-Miranda, "although she simply can't bake brownies like yours. So, Mrs. Smith, I think you should go pack your bags and I'll keep an eye on that pot." Alice-Miranda pulled up a stool to stand on.

Before she had time to change her mind, Cook handed the wooden spoon to Alice-Miranda and rushed to her room. She could hardly believe what she was doing—but it appeared that Alice-Miranda was not a child to be trifled with.

An hour later, Alice-Miranda heard the familiar *chop-chop-chop* of Birdy's whirring blades. It was a sound she had come to recognize well in her seven and one-quarter years. It usually meant that her parents were home and it always made her heart pound with excitement. Cyril landed the helicopter on the lower oval, and out hopped Mrs. Oliver, suitcase in hand. She wore her trademark blue suit, and her immovable brown curls sat immaculately in place as always. Hugh Kennington-Jones often teased that he thought Dolly must take her hair off at night and rest it on the nightstand. It was a running joke in the Highton-Smith-Kennington-Jones household that Dolly could well have been the lost sister of the

Queen. She had the same regal look—even when she was emerging from under the rotors of a helicopter. Within a minute Mrs. Smith had hopped in and Birdy hovered overhead, leaving Miss Grimm in her study wondering what that infernal noise was.

Mrs. Oliver was installed in the kitchen in a blink. Miss Grimm's dinner was delivered without a minute's delay and for the first time in years she ate everything on her plate and secretly wished for more. Mrs. Smith might have been the best brownie cook in the world, but Dolly Oliver could do cauliflower cheese better than anyone Alice-Miranda knew.

That evening, Alice-Miranda had her tea in the kitchen with Mrs. Oliver and Jacinta, then took herself off to her room to read. Miss Higgins came to tuck her in and say goodnight.

"Now, I'll be busy in the morning," Miss Higgins said distractedly as she smoothed the blanket, "but I shall leave Cook a note to ask her to wake you."

Alice-Miranda thought she should probably explain about Mrs. Smith's holiday, but Miss Higgins was in even more of a muddle than she had been earlier in the day, mumbling about unreliable house mistresses and mountains of work to be done. So Alice-Miranda decided that she wouldn't worry Miss

{39}

Higgins with the news—she would simply tell Miss Grimm in the morning instead.

She was really quite exhausted and looked forward to it being Sunday tomorrow. There would be lots of girls arriving back for the start of term and Alice-Miranda could hardly wait to meet them. She kissed Brummel Bear on the top of his head and drifted off to sleep.

Over in the headmistress's study, Miss Grimm's mind suddenly turned to the uncomfortable incident earlier in the day. She hadn't seen a child for years and this one was the most insistent little creature she could remember. Ever since their meeting, Miss Grimm had had a knot in her stomach that felt as if it were being steadily pulled at either end. She tried to put all thought of the brat out of her mind. It wouldn't do. Really, it wouldn't do at all. Her school was a tight ship and her job was to keep it that way.

Chapter 10

Alice-Miranda rolled over and rubbed her sleepy eyes. She yawned and stretched, then studied the pattern on the ceiling. She'd slept well, being quite used to staying in unfamiliar places when she traveled with her parents. The boardinghouse around her creaked and groaned as though it was waking up too. Her own house, Highton Hall, was full of grumbles in the morning—she liked to lie in bed and listen, imagining that the house was like an old friend full of stories. This morning she was wondering about the tales that this place, Grimthorpe House, could tell. Alice-Miranda picked up Brummel Bear and was about to ask him how he'd slept, when Mrs. Oliver popped her head around the door.

"Good morning, darling girl," she said with a smile.

"Hello, Mrs. Oliver," said Alice-Miranda, sitting up. "Did you sleep well?"

"Not too badly, although I have to say poor Mrs. Smith's bed is a brute. The woman will come back better than new if she just has some time on a decent mattress," Dolly said with a frown. "Now, you need to get yourself dressed, poppet, and come to the kitchen. And I'd best get a move on myself." Dolly bustled out of the room.

After breakfast—the most delicious eggs Benedict with smoked salmon—Alice-Miranda headed off to find Miss Grimm. She couldn't believe that even on a Sunday the headmistress would be too busy to speak with one of her students. Besides, Alice-Miranda was eager to let her know about Mrs. Smith's holiday.

The door to Miss Higgins's office was slightly ajar. Alice-Miranda knocked loudly and poked her head around the corner. There was no one inside, but a sliver of light came from Miss Grimm's study. Alice-Miranda scurried through the office and pushed open the study door, announcing herself with a cheerful "Hello, Miss Grimm, are you there?" She clicked the door shut behind her.

Miss Grimm was sitting at her desk, pen in hand, except this time she was not in her dressing-gown.

"Oh, there you are, Miss Grimm. I knew Miss Higgins had made a mistake with her note yesterday. I simply knew it wasn't true that you didn't see students—that would be ridiculous. Allow me to introduce myself properly. I know yesterday I caught you when you were obviously not ready to see anyone, but today, goodness, what a lovely suit. I think my mummy has one quite like it. Are you friends with Mr. Valentino too? I hope so. He simply is the most charming man and he has already told me that when I get married in a squillion years' time he wants to make me a gown. Dear me, I am talking a lot. My name is Alice-Miranda Highton-Smith-Kennington-Jones and I am truly honored to make your acquaintance, Miss Grimm." Alice-Miranda walked around the desk and held out her hand.

Miss Grimm swiveled slightly in her chair and peered over her spectacles, as if she were inspecting a grubby spill on the carpet. Alice-Miranda's hand hovered before finally, after what seemed more than a minute, Miss Grimm reached out. As their fingers met, Miss Grimm recoiled, pulling her hand away as though she'd been snapped at by an angry terrier. Alice-Miranda jumped in fright. The friction between them was like a bolt of lightning. Miss Grimm's face drained of color—she looked as if she had seen a ghost.

Alice-Miranda giggled. "It must be the dry wind. All that static electricity in the air. It makes my curls very frizzy." She twisted a strand of hair around her finger. Miss Grimm stared.

Alice-Miranda looked around the study and spied the empty breakfast tray on the side table. She inquired whether Miss Grimm had enjoyed her meal. Miss Grimm's eyes were fixed on Alice-Miranda but she seemed to nod ever so slightly.

"I am glad. You see, I hope you don't mind, but I have sent Mrs. Smith away to America for a holiday."

"You've done what?" Miss Grimm whispered. The color rose back into her cheeks.

"Well, I know I should have asked you yesterday and goodness, I did try, but you were not ready for visitors and when I came back there was a note saying that you were too busy to see anyone. I had arranged it already and I really didn't think you'd mind all that much as long as there was someone to cook your dinners. I'm sure you'll agree that Mrs. Oliver hasn't let us down yet. Last night's dinner was simply delicious and her eggs Benedict is one of the best I've ever tasted. You should have seen Mrs.

Smith. She was so excited when she flew off in Birdy."

Miss Grimm's mind wandered to the delectable cauliflower cheese from last evening. She couldn't remember eating anything so tasty in years. But there *was* still the troubling issue of this child and her impudence.

"Alice-Matilda, I will not have my students arranging things without my knowledge. I run a tight ship here at Winchesterfield-Downsfordvale and I will not have the likes of you ruining things," Miss Grimm hissed.

Alice-Miranda took a giant step backward. "I beg your pardon, Miss Grimm, it's Alice-Miranda, and I am sorry about the timing. I know I should have asked you first but I couldn't help myself when I saw how sad Mrs. Smith was about her grandchildren."

"Grandchildren? What are you talking about? The woman is barely old enough to be married, let alone to have grandchildren," Miss Grimm retorted.

"But she does have grandchildren. I've seen the photographs. And I beg your pardon, Miss Grimm; I'm no expert but I think Mrs. Smith is quite a lot older than you think."

At this stage Alice-Miranda felt it best to retreat to

the other side of the desk. She climbed up onto a chair, a safe distance from Miss Grimm.

"Anyway, Mrs. Smith will be back in two weeks and I'm sure that she will be so much happier. Holidays are very important. When was the last time you had a proper break away from the school, Miss Grimm? Somewhere you could read books and eat all manner of tasty things and lounge about doing absolutely nothing—if that's what you wanted."

"Frankly that's none of your business, Alice-Marika." Miss Grimm pulled her lips together very tightly. "I'm not interested in holidays. I'm interested in results. Winchesterfield-Downsfordvale didn't get its reputation by being on holiday." She thumped her fist on the desktop.

Alice-Miranda sat up straight in her chair. She drew in a deep breath. "Yes, Miss Grimm, I quite agree, but everyone needs a holiday at least once a year, and twice and three times is even better. Anyway, I don't think we need to talk about that anymore. There are a couple of other things I'm worried about."

Miss Grimm stared at the large leather-bound book in front of her.

"I really don't have time for this, Alice-Morganna. As far as I know there are no problems in my school, and if there were, Miss Higgins would alert me immediately. So, if you wouldn't mind, I have pressing business to attend to and you need to go and do whatever it is that students do." Miss Grimm began to write at a furious pace. She did not look up again.

Alice-Miranda knew that things were far worse than she had first feared. With or without Miss Grimm's help, there were jobs to be done. She slipped off the green leather chair and scampered to the door.

"Goodbye, Miss Grimm. I'll come and see you tomorrow when you have a minute, unless of course you'd like to take a walk in the garden later today. It's such a beautiful morning—Mummy says days like these are priceless treasures and I couldn't agree more," she said hopefully. She turned the brass doorknob and slipped into Miss Higgins's office, closing the door behind her.

"Hello, Miss Higgins." Alice-Miranda smiled.

Miss Higgins almost fell off her chair. It seemed that was something she did quite regularly.

"Alice-Miranda, wherever did you come from?" Miss Higgins asked anxiously.

"I've been having a lovely chat with Miss Grimm, but she's very busy now so I have to come back tomorrow."

"Didn't you get my letter?" Miss Higgins clenched her hands together.

"Yes, of course, but I thought you couldn't possibly be serious. It's just plain silly. Of course Miss Grimm sees people. How else would she know what goes on?"

Miss Higgins put her face in her hands—as though she were watching a really scary horror movie and something terrible was about to happen.

"Are you all right, Miss Higgins?" Alice-Miranda asked.

"Oh, Alice-Miranda, I can't believe that you ignored my letter. Whatever were you thinking going back in there again?" She clasped her hands so tightly they were beginning to turn white.

"It's all right, Miss Higgins. Miss Grimm and I had a good talk. I told her all about Mrs. Smith's holiday to America and that Mrs. Oliver was having a mar-velous time in the kitchen. I think she really liked Mrs. Oliver's cauliflower cheese."

"Whatever do you mean, Mrs. Smith's holiday?" Miss Higgins's face was ghostly white.

"Well, when I met Mrs. Smith yesterday she was very upset and it turns out that she was awfully sad that she had never gone on holiday to America to see her grandchildren. I asked her why—I mean, if it was because she couldn't afford it, I could well understand, but she said that wasn't the problem at all and she had lots of money saved up. The real reason was that Miss Grimm wouldn't let her take a holiday because there would be no one to cook her dinners. So I called Daddy and asked if I could borrow our cook, Mrs. Oliver, and he said yes. He and Mummy are going to town for a little while and so Mrs. Oliver wasn't busy anyway. And would you believe that Daddy was sending our plane to America for some special refitting and it was leaving yesterday afternoon?" Alice-Miranda paused and took a deep breath. "Anyway, it was too splendid an opportunity to miss and so Daddy sent Cyril, Birdy and Mrs. Oliver and then Mrs. Smith hopped into Birdy and away she flew. She'll be back in two weeks and I'm sure that she will be a different person. I can't imagine what it must be like for her never to see her grandchildren—I mean, most grandparents adore their grandchildren more than anything in the world. I know my granny does. She's always in trouble with Mummy for spoiling me. So I tried to tell Miss Grimm all about it yesterday but you left me the note and then I thought I would tell you last night but you were so busy, so I came today to catch her up."

"Oh dear." Miss Higgins looked close to tears. "Was she awfully mad?"

"No, not at all. We had a lovely chat about holidays."

Miss Higgins's forehead wrinkled like a dried apricot. "Did she really talk to you . . . about holidays?"

"Well, sort of. I told her that I think everyone needs to take holidays at least once a year and possibly twice, and even better still, three times. I don't think Miss Grimm's been on holidays for years," Alice-Miranda explained.

"You're right about that." Miss Higgins frowned. "Now, young lady, for your own good, I really must beg you not to visit Miss Grimm again. She doesn't like to be interrupted and I am afraid that having to deal with you will likely have put her into a very bad mood."

"I don't think she's in a bad mood," Alice-Miranda thought out loud. "Perhaps she just needs to get out more."

And with that Alice-Miranda skipped out of the office and down the hallway. She had far too many things occupying her mind to be worried about Miss Grimm's mood.

Chapter 11

Alice-Miranda took herself for a walk through the gardens. She was busy thinking about how to help Mr. Charles. Winchesterfield-Downsfordvale had beautiful grounds indeed. There were miles and miles of hedgerows, enormous oak trees and even a maze made entirely from tightly clipped box hedges, but it was true: there were no flowers. Alice-Miranda decided that it was like looking at the *Mona Lisa* without her smile. While it was almost perfect, there was just one thing that would make it even better. Alice-Miranda ran off to call her parents.

"Hello, Mummy," she said, beaming down the line.

"Oh, darling, it's so good to hear your voice." Her

mother did not even try to hide the fact that she was crying.

"Mummy, do stop crying. Are you and Daddy having an awfully bad time in town?" Alice-Miranda asked.

"No, of course not, sweetheart," her mother replied.

"So you're having a lovely time and I am too. Please don't be upset. Before you can even think about it, it will be midterm and I'll be home again," Alice-Miranda said sternly.

"I'm sorry, sweetheart," her mother replied.

"Mummy, there is something I thought you could help me with."

"Anything, darling."

"Well, you know the grounds here are lovely," Alice-Miranda began.

"Of course I do. I remember when I was a girl, the gardens were simply bursting with flowers: hollyhocks and daffodils, jonquils and irises. Every time one of the girls had a birthday, all her friends would make the most beautiful crown of flowers for her to wear all through the day and into the night."

"Well, I don't see how the girls could do that anymore."

"Why ever not, darling? Don't tell me some silly girl

was stung by a bee and now it's too dangerous?" Alice-Miranda's mother giggled.

"No, Mummy. It's just that, well . . . there are no flowers," Alice-Miranda whispered.

"Of course there are flowers. Winchesterfield-Downsfordvale is famous for its flowers. I remember kindly old Weatherly—he had the greenest thumbs."

"No, Mummy, I can assure you—there are *no* flowers."

"Why ever not?" Her mother sounded shocked.

"You see, I was talking to Mr. Charles—I think he must be Mr. Weatherly's son—and, well, he's in charge of the gardens now and is quite the gentlest giant of a man." Alice-Miranda hesitated. "He says that Miss Grimm doesn't like flowers. Can you imagine anyone not liking flowers? It sounds too silly for words. I'm sure she must be allergic." Alice-Miranda stated it as a known fact.

"Yes, I'm sure you're right, sweetheart. Imagine not liking flowers—they are one of life's purest pleasures."

"Mummy, do you think you and Daddy could help bring back the flowers?" Alice-Miranda asked.

"Yes, of course, darling. I'll send Mr. Greening and his team right away. Do you know, Daddy was telling me only yesterday that some very clever

{53}

people working in our development laboratory have just created the most perfect array of flowers with absolutely no smell at all? People with nasty hay fever and other allergies can have them in their gardens without getting all sneezy and wheezy."

Alice-Miranda beamed at her mother's words. "Oh, thank you, Mummy. I know that once Miss Grimm sees the flowers she'll just love them. I'd better go. There are loads of girls arriving and I want to meet every single one."

Alice-Miranda's heart leapt for joy.

Chapter 12

Alice-Miranda bounced off to the front of the school. There was a row of shiny cars lining the driveway. Girls of all shapes and sizes were gathering their suitcases and darting off this way and that. Alice-Miranda couldn't wait to meet them all and decided she must go at once to make friends. The first girl she came across was not much bigger than herself but with a brilliant crown of red hair. Her face was covered in freckles and she wore a particularly stylish pair of green spectacles.

"Hello," Alice-Miranda called out.

"Oh, hello," the red-haired girl called back.

"My name is Alice-Miranda Highton-Smith-

Kennington-Jones and I'm new." Alice-Miranda ran down the steps to help the girl with her rather large suitcase and enormous storage trunk. "I came yesterday."

"Well, my name is Millicent Jane McLoughlin-McTavish-McNoughton-McGill, but you can call me Millie."

Alice-Miranda smiled at Millie and offered to help take her bags to her room.

Millie was ten years old but very small for her age. By the time they had reached the house, Alice-Miranda felt that they had known each other for years. It turned out that they were sharing a room, a sure sign they would be very good friends indeed.

"My mother used to go to school here before me," Millie told Alice-Miranda. "And my grandmother before that and even my great-grandmother too."

"That's a coincidence. My mother, grandmother, great-grandmother and even more greats and all my aunts went here as well. I wonder if any of my family knew your family." Alice-Miranda bit her lip thoughtfully.

"I'm sure they did," said Millie. "Winchesterfield-Downsfordvale is not that big."

For the first time since she had arrived, Alice-Miranda's strange feeling was almost gone. It was as though the more girls arrived, the better things felt. There was simply no room left for strange feelings.

Alice-Miranda plonked Millie's suitcase down on the end of her bed.

"If you're all right here to unpack, I think I might go and meet some of the other girls."

"I'm fine," said Millie. "Thank you for helping me with everything. My mother is always so worried I might starve to death she packs extra treats in that wretched box." Millie shook her head and smiled.

"Well, I can guarantee that nobody will be starving tonight. Mrs. Oliver will see to that."

"Mrs. Oliver? What happened to Cook?" asked Millie.

"She's on holiday in America," Alice-Miranda said, as if it were the most usual thing in the world.

"On holiday!" Millie exclaimed. "But Cook never leaves Winchesterfield-Downsfordvale. Not even to go to the shops. She's such a crank pot and her food is *disgusting*!"

"Really? I can't imagine. Mrs. Smith baked the most delicious brownies—the best I have ever tasted—and she gave me a glass of milk too." Now it was Alice-Miranda's turn to frown.

"She cooked what? And she gave you a glass of milk? What's been going on around here?" Millie stopped fiddling with the zips on her suitcase and stared at Alice-Miranda.

"I'll explain it all later." Alice-Miranda's feet were twitching with her eagerness to meet all the other girls. She said goodbye to Millie and left her to unpack.

Chapter 13

Alice-Miranda ran back to the driveway. There seemed to be quite a traffic jam. She raced around to the front steps of Winchesterfield Manor to get a better view. There in the middle of the road was quite the longest and shiniest limousine she had ever seen.

"Goodness!" Alice-Miranda exclaimed to herself. "What an enormous car. I wonder whose that is."

Behind her a tiny voice answered.

"It's Alethea Goldsworthy's, and if you know what's good for you you'll stay right out of her way."

Alice-Miranda turned to see who was speaking but the girl had already scurried out of sight. Oh well, she thought, I should go and introduce myself. She can't be that bad.

Alethea's chauffeur was a hapless-looking fellow with a very large tummy and rather short legs. He was wrestling the most enormous suitcase Alice-Miranda had ever seen out of the trunk and onto a luggage cart.

Suddenly, from inside the car came a howling noise, like a wolf with a thorn in its paw.

Alice-Miranda ran to see what the matter was. She wrenched open the back door and was almost hit by a flying bottle.

"Goodness, what's wrong?" Alice-Miranda ducked her head just in time, as another bottle of soft drink exploded onto the gravel drive behind her.

"Where's my mineral water?" the girl screamed, as she threw bottle after bottle out of the limousine's minibar. Alice-Miranda climbed inside the car. Luckily she had very good reflexes and managed to dodge the liquid missiles.

"Hello, can I do anything to help?" she asked. "My name is Alice-Miranda Highton-Smith-Kennington-Jones and I'm very pleased to meet you. It's Alethea, isn't it?"

"Get out of my car," the girl snapped, and threw a half-empty bottle of cola at Alice-Miranda's head.

Fortunately she was not a very good shot and it fell noisily to the floor.

"It can't be all that bad. I'm sure we can find some mineral water in there somewhere." Alice-Miranda leaned over to look inside.

"Get out of my car," the girl insisted. "I don't want you in here and if you don't leave this instant I will call the police." Alethea's eyes narrowed to angry slits.

"Well, that's just plain nonsense," Alice-Miranda said. "Why would you do that? I'm just trying to help. Besides, no police officer is going to waste a minute of their time on a silly old tantrum."

"GET OUT!" Alethea screeched. At that very moment everyone on the driveway stopped. Chauffeurs were frozen to the spot, girls stood perfectly still (except for some trembling knees), parents stopped fussing.

Miss Higgins, who had been rushing about from car to car, greeting girls and helping with their things, stopped in her tracks. "Oh dear, this is going to be bad, very bad," she whispered to herself.

In the back of the limousine Alice-Miranda was considering her options.

"Please, please, please stop yelling," she soothed in her calmest voice. She couldn't believe that Alethea

Goldsworthy made even more noise than Jacinta Headlington-Bear.

"I WILL NOT!" Alethea threw a bottle of what looked to be very posh champagne out the door. It smashed onto the gravel, exploding into thousands of tiny bubbles.

"Alethea, that's a terrible waste. Dom Pérignon is frightfully expensive," Alice-Miranda sighed.

"I don't care. I want my mineral water. Daddy said Harold would put in ten bottles and he hasn't even put in one. I hate him."

"Who?" asked Alice-Miranda, interrupting Alethea's rant.

"Daddy. No, Harold. No, I hate them both. They never do what they say they will and I need my mineral water."

"I've got some in my storage trunk," Alice-Miranda offered. "You can have it if you like. It's from Switzerland."

"Why would I want your disgusting mineral water—*from Switzerland*?" Alethea mimicked Alice-Miranda.

"Well, it's there if you'd like it. I think I might go and meet some of the other girls now." Alice-Miranda slid across the seat toward the open door. "It's been very nice to meet you, Alethea."

"Where do you think you're going?" the girl screeched.

"Well, you told me to get out of the car and so that's what I'm going to do." Alice-Miranda smiled.

"You can't go until I say so." Alethea crossed her arms and glared at the smaller girl.

"But you did say so, just a moment ago." Alice-Miranda bit her lip. She'd never come across anyone quite so contrary.

"Well, now you have to stay." Alethea launched herself at the door and pulled it closed. "You have to do everything I say."

"That's silly." Alice-Miranda smiled again. "I think Miss Grimm will have something to say about that."

"Why would she?" Alethea snapped. "She never comes out of her study. I run this school. I'm in charge and you have to do everything I say."

"I spoke to Miss Grimm just yesterday and we had a lovely conversation all about holidays," Alice-Miranda replied.

"I don't believe you!" Alethea grabbed Alice-Miranda's tiny arm and twisted it hard.

"Ow, that hurts," Alice-Miranda squeaked. "Please let go."

"You're a liar. Miss Grimm doesn't talk to anyone, especially you," Alethea spat.

Suddenly the door flew open and Miss Higgins appeared.

"Hello, Alethea. Oh, there you are, Alice-Miranda. I've been looking for you."

Alethea quickly let go of Alice-Miranda's arm and slid back along the seat.

"Come along, you need to hop out, Alethea. There are other girls arriving and your car is blocking the whole driveway." Miss Higgins caught sight of the bright red mark on Alice-Miranda's forearm.

"Dear me, Alice-Miranda, what have you done to yourself?" Miss Higgins's lips drew tightly together.

"Oh, I must have bumped it when I was helping Millie with her storage trunk." Alice-Miranda smiled. Alethea glared.

Alice-Miranda hopped out of the car with Alethea close behind.

"If you tell anyone, you're dead," Alethea hissed.

"What was that, Alethea?" Miss Higgins asked.

"Nothing, Miss Higgins. I was just telling Alice-Miranda what a great school Winchesterfield-Downsfordvale is." She gave a smile as sweet as sugar on cinnamon doughnuts.

"Come along, Alice-Miranda, there are some other girls I would like you to meet," Miss Higgins directed. Alethea followed closely behind.

Miss Higgins noticed Alice-Miranda's oversized shadow and turned around.

"Alethea, what are you doing? You need to go and help your poor driver with that enormous mountain of luggage. Goodness knows what you have brought back with you," Miss Higgins tutted.

Alethea skulked off back to her car. On the way, she turned to Alice-Miranda.

"See you later, Alice-Miranda." Her smile was petrifying.

"It was nice to meet you, Alethea. And if you do want some mineral water, I'm happy to share mine." Alice-Miranda smiled back.

"I'm glad that you're all right." Miss Higgins held Alice-Miranda's tiny hand. "Alethea can be a little tricky and when I heard that awful screeching, well, I was afraid."

"It's all right, Miss Higgins. Alethea is just . . . I suppose you could call it complicated. Perhaps she's sad about leaving her parents and having to come back to school? Who knows, but there's always a reason why people behave the way they do. I'm sure that underneath it all she's a very sweet girl."

Miss Higgins was cross with herself. Alice-Miranda was right, of course. One shouldn't think badly of others. Everyone deserved a chance. It was just that

Alethea had earned herself a reputation for being difficult in the extreme over the past few years. But if this seven-year-old could see the good in Alethea then she should be ashamed of herself for thinking that Alethea was beyond help.

Miss Higgins squeezed Alice-Miranda's hand and gazed down at her sweet brown eyes. In the past she had always been careful not to show favoritism to any of the girls. But there was something about Alice-Miranda that just made her want to scoop the girl up and hug her.

Chapter 14

Alice-Miranda spent the rest of Sunday meeting lots of other girls. She was determined to remember as many names as possible and made up rhymes to help her. There was Madeline Bloom *in the very next room* and Susannah Dare *with curly hair,* Ivory Hicks *who did magic tricks* and Ashima Divall *who was beautifully tall.* Alice-Miranda asked loads of questions about the teachers and the subjects and all of the wonderful things that they would do during the term. Everyone was helpful but they all seemed to say the same thing—that the teachers were terribly strict and school wasn't much fun.

"Hello, Millie!" Alice-Miranda exclaimed when at last she bounded back to her own room.

Millie was sprawled out on her bed reading. She looked up and placed her book on the bedside table. "Hello there. So have you met everyone?"

"I don't think I've met them all, but quite a few. Everyone seemed rather happy about being back at school. Well, except for Alethea. She was having a little tantrum about some mineral water." Alice-Miranda laughed.

"Oh good grief. Sorry about that. I meant to warn you to stay out of her way." Millie sat up and crossed her legs.

Alice-Miranda sat on the end of her own bed, facing Millie. "It's okay. I told her she could have my mineral water if she wanted it."

"Oh no. You shouldn't have done that, Alice-Miranda. She'll make you her personal slave, like she does with all of the new girls."

"Well, that's plain silly. She tried to tell me that I had to do everything she said and I told her that I was sure Miss Grimm would have something to say about that," Alice-Miranda replied.

Millie's brows knitted together and she covered her face with her hands. "You shouldn't have said anything to her. Now she'll definitely want you. The best way to get on with Alethea is to avoid her completely. And stay away from her gang too. There are three of them and they will do their best to wear you down. Danika, Lizzy and Shelby—Alethea's three marionettes and, might I add, some of the nastiest puppets you will ever meet." Millie had lowered her voice and Alice-Miranda was leaning forward to hear her.

"Really? They can't be as bad as all that . . . can they?" Alice-Miranda asked.

"That bad and worse. Last year they broke into the science lab, stole some Condy's crystals and turned the swimming pool purple. Workers came to drain the water and then Alethea told Miss Reedy that she had heard Mr. Plumpton laughing and telling Charlie that when he was a boy, he and some friends had done the exact same thing to their local swimming pool. Miss Reedy said that whether Mr. Plumpton did it or not, it was his fault for talking about such ridiculous things in places where impressionable young girls might hear. It must have been reported to Miss Grimm. He was almost sacked, you know."

"Oh." Alice-Miranda touched her finger to her lip thoughtfully.

"Then there was an awful tragedy with Madeline Bloom's rabbit. Someone opened the hutch door and he got out into the garden. That wouldn't have been a problem except that Mr. Evershed from the village brought his dogs and ferrets up that day to hunt some wild rabbits near the river. You can imagine what happened when they caught sight of poor little Cadbury sitting out in the middle of the lawn just minding his own business. Alethea saw the whole thing and seemed to enjoy telling everyone the gory details. Poor Madeline had to stay in the infirmary for a week and when she finally did stop crying, Alethea sent her a note saying how sorry she was." Millie's face was very serious as she said this.

"Well, that was kind, wasn't it?" Alice-Miranda asked hopefully.

"It might have been if she hadn't written it on a card with a picture of a terrier on the front. The caption said *Life gone to the dogs?* Then inside the terrier had its head stuck down a rabbit hole with a cutaway view of the poor rabbits inside cowering in the corner. The message said, *Cheer up, it could be worse.*"

"Oh, that's awful," Alice-Miranda gasped. "How could she?"

"That's what everyone said."

"Did anyone take the card to Miss Grimm? Surely Alethea must have got into trouble?" Alice-Miranda asked.

"Why would anyone take it to Grimm? She never comes out of her study. I've never even seen her and I've been here for two years," Millie snorted.

Alice-Miranda unfurled her legs and spread out on the bed. "When I arrived Miss Higgins told me that Miss Grimm didn't see students but I didn't believe her. I've seen Miss Grimm twice now. I was rather hoping to catch her again tomorrow." Alice-Miranda picked up Brummel Bear and stroked the top of his fuzzy head.

"That's outrageous!" Millie exclaimed. "What's she like? I've heard that she's got the most frightening black eyes." Millie leaned in closer, eager for more terrible tales.

"Well, she's very tall. The first time I saw her she was in her dressing-gown and I suppose she looked like, I don't know, perhaps like my aunt Charlotte, really—when she's lounging about at home with her hair not done properly. When I saw her this morning she was dressed in a very elegant suit—rather like one my mummy has. Her hair was pulled back into a lovely French roll."

"I can't believe you've seen her," Millie gasped, "and in her dressing-gown too! Was she terribly scary?"

"I wouldn't say so. I think Mummy would call her stylishly severe, but I suspect she's actually quite pretty, really. Mummy and Daddy have some friends who are far more fearsome. Lord Gisborne is the crustiest old fellow in the world—always being cross and saying that children should be seen and not heard. Anyway, I don't think Miss Grimm's scary, I think she's sad," Alice-Miranda concluded.

"Whatever did you talk about?" The color had drained from Millie's freckles and she looked as though she might faint.

"I told her about Mrs. Smith's holiday to America. I know I should have asked her, but it all happened so quickly and then Mrs. Oliver came, and her food is delish, so in the end I really don't think she was that upset at all. I asked Miss Grimm when she had last had a good holiday—I really think she needs one. Anyway, I asked her if she wanted to come for a walk in the garden later today but I think she's rather busy. I said I would pop in again tomorrow."

"Gosh, wait until the other girls hear that you've seen Grimm—not only seen her but talked to her too. That's the stuff legends are made of, Alice-Miranda. And I can tell you now, that's another thing Alethea will hate you for." Millie smiled and squeezed her knees up under her chin.

Alice-Miranda changed the subject. "Well, if Miss Grimm doesn't see anyone, then surely Madeline or one of the girls must have told a teacher about Alethea's horrible card?"

"Madeline told Miss Reedy but she didn't do anything. She just made an excuse, as usual. She said that perhaps Alethea was trying to cheer her up and of course she wouldn't have sent that particular card just to upset her. It must have been a misunderstanding." Millie grabbed the hairbrush from beside her bed and started to untangle her thick red mane.

"Do the teachers usually make excuses for her?" Alice-Miranda asked.

"Haven't you been for a walk around the school?" Millie inquired.

"Yes, of course. It's beautiful," said Alice-Miranda, wondering why Millie was changing the subject.

"And what's the loveliest building here?" Millie asked.

"Well, it would be hard to say, really," Alice-Miranda thought aloud, "it's all gorgeous. Winchesterfield Manor is very grand. I suppose the library looks rather special too." She nodded.

"Hard to believe that it's just a year old." Millie laid the brush back down and began to twist a strand of hair around her finger.

"A year!" Alice-Miranda gasped. "But it looks like it's been here for at least a hundred years."

"Did you happen to read the plaque next to the entry?"

"No," Alice-Miranda replied. "Why? What does it say?"

"Well, you might understand a little better about our dear Alethea when you read it," Millie teased.

"Tell me what it says," Alice-Miranda begged.

"Come on, let's go for a walk and I'll show you." Millie spun her legs to the side of the bed and slipped on her shoes.

Chapter 15

Alice-Miranda and Millie headed out of Grimthorpe House, down the path and across the enormous flagstone courtyard. The library loomed majestically, attached to the ancient Winchesterfield Manor by an intricate archway. Its sandstone walls glowed yellow in the afternoon sun.

"There—on the wall." Millie pointed at the giant brass plaque beside the entry.

Alice-Miranda read aloud: "'The Goldsworthy Library. Built entirely from moneys donated by the Goldsworthy family in honor of their beloved only daughter, Alethea, a student at Winchesterfield-Downsfordvale Academy for Proper Young Ladies.'"

Alice-Miranda gasped. "So that's why she thinks she rules the school."

"There aren't too many girls here whose fathers could donate the money for all that." Millie waved her arms in the air like a magician's assistant.

"No, I don't suppose there are," Alice-Miranda agreed. "But it doesn't give her the right to be unkind."

The two girls stood side by side studying the building in front of them. Suddenly they heard raised voices. It sounded like a man and a woman arguing.

"Quick!" Millie grabbed Alice-Miranda's arm and pulled her behind a huge stone urn guarding the entrance to the library.

"What are you doing?" Alice-Miranda asked.

"Shh." Millie put her hand over Alice-Miranda's mouth.

The adults were now standing on the other side of the urn. Alice-Miranda peered out to watch what was happening but Millie kept a tight grip on her arm.

The tallest and thinnest woman Alice-Miranda had ever seen was having a very vigorous discussion with possibly the roundest man she had ever clapped eyes on.

"I refuse to do it. I just won't." The man shook his sausage-like forefinger at the woman.

"You must do as you're told, Mr. Plumpton, or you'll be out on your ear," the lady said with a frown.

"But I can't teach drama. I don't know the first thing about Shakespeare. I'm the science teacher and *I have been* the science teacher for thirty years," the fat man sighed.

"I'm not exactly happy about the situation myself. I don't know how I am expected to take on the junior mathematics program when I have only ever taught senior English. Frankly, I don't need any further challenges—my life is already busy enough keeping on top of the girls' behavior."

"You know, Miss Reedy, that science is my passion. It is my life's work and the thing that I love more than any other. Well, perhaps second only to one other." Mr. Plumpton's nose glowed red.

Miss Reedy blushed and looked away.

"It's not fair—she's getting worse each year and I won't put up with it for much longer." Mr. Plumpton stamped his foot.

"Come along, Josiah, let's have some tea," Miss Reedy soothed. The couple disappeared through the doorway at the end of the veranda.

"Why did we have to hide?" Alice-Miranda asked as she and Millie stood up. "I would have liked to meet them."

"Believe me, you shouldn't be in a hurry to meet Miss Reedy," Millie replied. "Mr. Plumpton is all right most of the time."

"Why? What does she do? Apart from teach English."

"Miss Reedy looks after discipline and she takes her job *very* seriously. Last year I got three detentions in a week. The first time because my hair ribbon was untied, the second time because my shoelace was undone and then the last one was because my socks had slipped a centimeter below my knees."

"That *is* tough," Alice-Miranda agreed. "But they both seemed so unhappy. It sounds a bit silly to have teachers who love their work being given subjects they don't know anything about. I'll tell Miss Grimm as soon as I see her. Surely she can fix things."

"I can't imagine telling Miss Grimm anything," Millie replied. "And I wouldn't worry about Miss Reedy and Mr. Plumpton—I'm sure they can look after themselves."

"Come on," Alice-Miranda suggested. "Let's go and see Mrs. Oliver. I wonder what she's cooking for our dinner."

The girls raced off to the kitchen, entering through the back screen door.

"Hello, Mrs. Oliver." Alice-Miranda ran the few

steps toward her and was welcomed like a much-loved granddaughter.

"Hello, my darling girl." Mrs. Oliver cuddled Alice-Miranda into her starched white apron. "Have you come to see what I might be whipping up for your dinner?" she asked in her lilting Irish brogue. "Or are you planning to pilfer some more of my cakes?"

"Cakes?" Alice-Miranda looked puzzled. "What cakes?"

Mrs. Oliver shook her head. "I baked this afternoon and I could have sworn I left four chocolate cakes sitting over there on the bench and now there's . . ."

"Only three," Alice-Miranda finished. "Well, I can assure you that it wasn't us."

"Oh, I know it wasn't you. I just wonder—perhaps I didn't count properly. . . ." Mrs. Oliver's voice trailed off.

Alice-Miranda raised her button nose and drew in a deep breath. "Well, whatever's for dinner smells delicious. Let me guess. . . . I think it must be your famous Irish stew with boiled potatoes. Am I right?" She climbed up onto a small footstool and lifted the lid of the gigantic pot.

"You know me far too well, lass. And who is this you've brought along with you?"

"Oh, sorry, Millie—how rude of me. Mrs. Oliver,

this is Millicent Jane McLoughlin-McTavish-McNoughton-McGill, but you can call her Millie."

"I am very pleased to make your acquaintance, Miss Millie." Mrs. Oliver hugged her—not quite as tightly as she had Alice-Miranda, but with genuine affection nonetheless.

"Now, my dear, would you perhaps be related to Ambrose McLoughlin-McTavish?" Mrs. Oliver inquired.

"Yes. He's my grandfather. How do you know him?" Millie's green eyes sparkled.

"Well, let's just say that a very long time ago we were grand friends. How is the dear man?" Mrs. Oliver placed a huge wooden spoon into the vat of stew and stirred three times.

"He's as gorgeous as ever—would you like me to send your regards?"

"I'd like that very much," said Mrs. Oliver. "And now, my poppets, you need to run along and get washed up for your dinner. According to these here instructions from Mrs. Smith I need to have this meal on the table at exactly six p.m. or there will be trouble. I also need to get Miss Grimm's dinner over to her and I haven't seen hide nor hair of Miss Higgins all afternoon."

"We'll take it over if you like," Alice-Miranda offered.

"It's a heavy tray, my dear. I don't know that you'd be able to manage," said Mrs. Oliver.

Alice-Miranda ran over to the bench where Miss Grimm's tea tray was set up. "Do you know what this needs?" she quizzed.

"Some food," Millie laughed.

"Apart from food, I think it needs a lovely little flower to brighten it up." Once more Alice-Miranda grabbed the footstool and began opening and closing cupboard doors in her search.

"What are you looking for, lass?" asked Mrs. Oliver, turning from the stove.

"A vase. Look, here's one." She pulled the dusty piece of crystal from the cupboard. "Gosh, it doesn't look like it's been used for years!" Alice-Miranda exclaimed, and gave it a good wash.

"I hate to upset your plans, but haven't you noticed that Winchesterfield-Downsfordvale doesn't have any flowers?" Millie grabbed a towel and started drying the soapy bud vase.

"I know. But that's all about to change. I had a lovely cup of tea with Mr. Charles yesterday and he told me all about the flowers. He was so sad that there are none here, and he's absolutely right. Anyway, I called Mummy and she's arranging to send our gardener, Mr. Greening, and his team up tomorrow to give the place a complete makeover. Mr. Charles does have some lovely orchids in the greenhouse, though."

"You've done what?" Millie almost dropped the vase.

"Mummy said that when she was here, the girls made beautiful crowns of flowers for each other's birthdays. When I told her that there were no flowers anywhere she thought that perhaps Miss Grimm must be allergic. Anyway, some very clever scientists who work for Daddy and Mummy have just perfected a whole new strain of flowers that have no smell. So they are wonderful for people who are allergic." Alice-Miranda was speaking so quickly Millie was having a hard time keeping up.

"And Miss Grimm's allergic to flowers?" Millie placed the dry vase onto the tea tray and looked quizzically at her friend.

"Well, I should think so. I can't imagine another reason why she wouldn't want flowers at Winchesterfield-Downsfordvale, can you?" Alice-Miranda pushed the stool she had been standing on back underneath the kitchen bench.

Millie shrugged. "No, unless she's just mean and awful and doesn't like anything pretty."

"That can't be it at all. Miss Grimm's not mean and awful," Alice-Miranda replied.

"Goodness me, girl, you are quite the organizer," Mrs. Oliver interjected. "If you would like to pop over and see your Mr. Charles, perhaps he can cut you a lovely little orchid and then if you think you can manage, the two of you can take Miss Grimm's tea tray over to her study."

The color suddenly drained from Millie's freckly cheeks.

"What's the matter, Miss Millie?" Mrs. Oliver asked.

"Well, I was telling Alice-Miranda earlier that I've been here for two years now and I have never seen Miss Grimm," Millie replied.

"Don't be afraid, lass. She's just a lady like any other. She must be very busy and she seems to do a cracking job of looking after this school. I'm sure she has her reasons for keeping out of sight."

Alice-Miranda skipped out the kitchen door with Millie scampering after her. When they reached the greenhouse Mr. Charles was busily potting some hedge cuttings and didn't hear the girls come in.

"Hello, Mr. Charles," Alice-Miranda said, beaming.

"Oh, hello there, young lady. I was rather hoping to see you today." He smiled and lifted Alice-Miranda up onto the bench, where she sat dangling her legs.

"Hello, Charlie." Millie was hesitant. She'd never been into the greenhouse before.

"Miss Millie. Did you enjoy the holidays?" Charlie inquired.

"Yes, Charlie, thank you." Millie's face broke into a smile.

"I've come to ask a favor and to tell you some rather wonderful news," Alice-Miranda began.

"What is it you have to tell me?" Charlie asked as he continued his potting.

"Well, first of all, do you think it would be possible to have just one of your lovely orchids?" Alice-Miranda's brown eyes smiled irresistibly.

"I don't see why not." Charlie glanced up. "Just because Miss Grimm don't like flowers shouldn't mean that everyone misses out."

"And secondly, I called Mummy and told her about there being no flowers and she said that Winchesterfield-Downsfordvale was famous for its flowers and that was just silly. So tomorrow Mr. Greening and his team will be here to help you plant thousands of flowers. Special ones with no perfume so they won't upset Miss Grimm's allergies."

Charlie dropped the pot he was planting. "But we don't know for sure that she's allergic," he said, and gulped.

"Mummy and I decided for certain that the only reason Miss Grimm wouldn't like flowers is that she must be allergic. Who doesn't like flowers?" Alice-Miranda began. "And then when I was asking Millie and Mrs. Oliver they both agreed that it couldn't really be anything else."

"Well, all I know for sure is that she doesn't want any flowers. Have you told her about your plan?" Charlie suddenly looked more like a schoolboy than a grown man.

"Well, no, not yet. I thought it would be a lovely surprise." Alice-Miranda's eyes sparkled.

Charlie's face fell. "I'll lose me job over it, that's what'll happen."

"Of course you won't. Don't you worry about a thing, Mr. Charles. I'll go and see Miss Grimm and I'll make sure that everything's fine." Alice-Miranda jumped off the bench and headed toward the orchids. "Now, which one of these beauties may we have?" she asked, craning her neck to see.

Chapter 16

Alice-Miranda and Millie carried Miss Grimm's tea tray as though they were in charge of the Queen's own supper. At one point Millie stumbled on a stone and for a second it looked as if the whole thing might topple into the garden.

"That was close," Alice-Miranda gasped as they regained control of the tray.

As the girls neared the office Alice-Miranda wondered if Miss Higgins would be very cross. She hoped she mightn't be too upset, seeing as how they were saving her the bother of delivering Miss Grimm's supper.

The door to Miss Higgins's office was closed. There was a sign hanging from the knob.

Dear Girls and Staff,

I have been called away to attend to family business. If you require assistance please see Miss Reedy or Mr. Plumpton in the teachers' study. First door down the hallway to the left.

Kindest regards,
Miss Louella Higgins
Personal Secretary to the
   Headmistress
Winchesterfield-Downsfordvale
   Academy for Proper Young Ladies

Alice-Miranda was intrigued. "I wonder what sort of family business Miss Higgins has been called to?"

"Alethea's pillows probably need plumping or she's run out of wardrobe space," Millie laughed.

"Surely not!" Alice-Miranda exclaimed. "Miss Higgins has far more important jobs than fussing over Alethea."

Millie raised an eyebrow. "I wouldn't bet on it."

Alice-Miranda instructed Millie to set the tray

down on the table outside Miss Higgins's door. She clasped the brass knob and to her surprise found the door unlocked. Alice-Miranda dragged a chair over to prop open the door and the girls carefully picked up the tray and walked inside, setting it down again on the corner of Miss Higgins's desk.

"I always wondered what it was like in here." Millie walked around inspecting this and that. She picked up a small brass elephant from the corner of Miss Higgins's desk.

"We really shouldn't touch anything," said Alice-Miranda. "I can't believe you've never been in here. Miss Higgins is so lovely, and helpful too."

"Well, I suppose I've just never really had any reason to come in here." Millie walked around, her forefinger skimming the desk as though she were a maid checking for dust.

There was a sliver of light coming from under the door to Miss Grimm's study.

"So is that where she is?" whispered Millie, her face turning ghostly white.

"Who? Oh, you mean Miss Grimm." Alice-Miranda nodded. "I'll knock and see if she's about. If she's not in we can just leave the tray on her desk. She must be expecting it soon anyway."

"Are you sure?" Millie whispered. "Perhaps we

could just leave the tray out here and push a note under the door."

"Don't be silly. I'd hate for Miss Grimm's dinner to get cold. I can't imagine she'd be very pleased with Mrs. Oliver. There's nothing to be afraid of, really," Alice-Miranda said reassuringly.

She tapped gently on the door. There was no answer, so she turned the handle and popped her head inside.

"Hello, Miss Grimm? Are you there?"

She was greeted by silence.

"Come on, let's just take the tray in and go," Millie urged from behind.

"Helloooo, Miss Grimm?" Alice-Miranda took a few steps inside. Although it was summer, a fire danced in the hearth. The black marble mantel glinted darkly. Miss Grimm's enormous desk sat proudly to the left of the double entrance doors. To the right were two dark green leather chesterfield lounges and a high-backed armchair in a stern navy stripe. On the facing wall a solid mahogany bookcase filled with classic tales groaned under its weight of wisdom. It struck Alice-Miranda that the room quite resembled her father's study. Even the curtains, though elegant in design, were heavy and dark.

Alice-Miranda spied another door at the opposite

end of the room which looked to be slightly ajar. She headed toward it.

"Alice-Miranda, come back!" Millie whispered urgently.

"Miss Grimm. Helloooo. We've brought your tea tray. It smells utterly delicious. Are you there?" Alice-Miranda called.

She was about to put her hand on the knob when suddenly the door burst open. She was almost bowled over but managed to jump out of the way just in time. Over by the other door Millie trembled like jelly.

"What are you doing in here?" Miss Grimm demanded.

"Oh, hello, Miss Grimm. There you are. I was rather hoping to see you in the garden this afternoon but I imagine, being the start of term and all, that you have loads of things to do. Life is always so busy for grown-ups. Millie and I have brought your dinner, and it's a lovely one too."

Miss Grimm sniffed the air. The faint waft of Irish stew caused her stomach to groan.

"Was that your tummy rumbling? You'll love this— it's Mrs. Oliver's famous family recipe. No one in the world makes a better Irish stew. Even when I went to Ireland last year with Mummy and Daddy and we went to this ever so posh restaurant with Earl O'Connor, the Irish stew wasn't as good as our Dolly's. Of course, I didn't tell them so because that wouldn't have been polite." Alice-Miranda smiled. "Anyway, Millie and I will just bring the tray through for you. Where would you like it?" Alice-Miranda thought she could hear a very loud clock but realized when she turned around that it was actually Millie's knees knocking together.

"How dare you enter my study without my permission, Alice-Matilda!" Miss Grimm drew her lips together tightly. She stood with her hands on her suited hips. Her eyebrows furrowed fiercely above eyes the color of coal.

"Please, Miss Grimm, I'm Alice-Miranda, not Matilda. I know it must be terribly hard to remember all of the girls' names. I met so many girls today I knew that if I didn't make up some rhymes I would never remember them. Perhaps it could help you too. So there's Madeline Bloom *in the very next room* and Susannah Dare *with curly hair,* Ivory Hicks *who does magic tricks* and Ashima Divall *who is beautifully tall.* Maybe you could remember me with something like Alice-Miranda *out on the veranda.* Miranda's a hard name to put rhymes with and if you tried to do it for Highton-Smith-Kennington-Jones you might not remember it at all." Alice-Miranda skipped back to fetch the tea tray.

"Who's on the veranda?" Miss Grimm snarled.

"Well, I'm not really on the veranda but it's just a way to remember my name," Alice-Miranda laughed. "We'll just get your dinner, Miss Grimm," she called as she and Millie steadily lifted the tray and walked toward the huge mahogany desk.

"Over there!" Miss Grimm commanded, her eyes wide and mouth gaping as she pointed at the low table in front of the chesterfields.

"That's a lovely spot to have your dinner," said Alice-Miranda. "This is such a grand room. Although it would look even better with some flowers. Just look at how that orchid brightens the whole place." Alice-Miranda nodded at the tea tray with the single orchid stem. "And some photographs. That's what you need. Some pictures of your family and perhaps some of your adventures on holiday. My daddy's study is quite like this, but I couldn't think what the difference was and then it just came to me. Daddy has tons of photos of me and Mummy and some of the places we've visited and all of our special friends. That's what's missing. . . ."

"OUT!" Miss Grimm roared, pointing a long red talon toward the door. "Where is that woman? Probably run off to get married, I should think . . . useless good-for-nothing," she murmured under her breath.

"Oh, that's silly, Miss Grimm. Miss Higgins wouldn't go off and get married without inviting you. She's attending to some sort of unexpected emergency," explained Alice-Miranda.

Miss Grimm couldn't believe this child. What a ridiculous notion—that she might be invited to a wedding. Let alone that she might actually *go*.

"That will be all, Alice-Mat—Miranda." She gritted her teeth.

Millie had already escaped to Miss Higgins's office. Alice-Miranda turned and smiled at Miss Grimm.

"Enjoy your dinner, Miss Grimm. I will see you tomorrow—I'm so excited about the start of school I don't think I'll be able to sleep very much at all. I hope you can sleep." Alice-Miranda straightened a cushion and began to retreat to the main doors.

"Of course I can sleep. Why wouldn't I?" Miss Grimm said, thinking aloud. She hadn't really meant to ask a question at all.

"Well, it must be terribly exciting to see all of the girls after they've been away on such a long holiday. All those lovely adventures to hear about and so many exciting things to look forward to. And the teachers are no doubt thrilled to be back with the girls and teaching their favorite subjects. Oh, that reminds me. I saw Miss Reedy and Mr. Plumpton earlier and they were both very upset. Apparently they have been directed to teach subjects they are not at all used to, and, well, it does seem a little silly to have Mr. Plumpton, a science teacher with such enthusiasm for science, teaching drama. He says he knows nothing about *that* at all. And Miss Reedy said that she's going to be taking junior mathematics and I understand she usually teaches senior English. Is it possible that someone made a mistake with that?" Alice-Miranda looked Miss Grimm right in the eye as she spoke.

"A mistake! A mistake! How dare you suggest such a thing? I don't make mistakes, Alice-Miranda. They will do as they are told and I will hear no more of it." Miss Grimm's mouth was agape, showing a gleaming set of teeth to rival an Amazonian piranha.

"Well, perhaps they could come and talk to you about it. It does seem awfully silly and they are both so . . . passionate. I'll tell them to make a time with Miss Higgins tomorrow. Well . . . I'm sorry to prattle on, Miss Grimm. Your dinner will be getting cold and it really is much better nice and warm. See you tomorrow." And with that Alice-Miranda turned on her heel and skipped out the door, pulling it closed behind her.

Miss Grimm strode forward and snapped the lock. Her mind was racing. This child, this tiny little girl with chocolate curls and eyes as round as saucers, was turning her life on its head. Putting all sorts of nonsensical ideas into her mind. Photographs—what need did she have of photographs? A sharp memory invaded her thoughts. She pushed it away as quickly as it had come. People she loved, friends and holidays. Being excited about school. Good grief—there was nothing more dull than being at school.

Chapter 17

That night Ophelia Grimm tossed and turned in her bed. The canopy heaved as she fought round after round with her feather pillows. Her sleep was alive with dreams. Dreams of children, of girls playing and laughing. The clanging of the school bell and a hundred pairs of feet running to their classrooms.

She awoke suddenly as though falling from a hole in the sky. Her brow was peppered with perspiration; her heart ready to leap from her chest. The first shards of daylight entered the room but it took several minutes for her to realize that she was still in her very own bed where she had slept for the past fifteen years.

Her mind was racing. What did it all mean? She

hadn't dreamt for years, certainly not about children. It was that child. It was Alice-Miranda or whatever her ridiculous name was. It was her fault and she had to be dealt with. Why Ophelia had agreed to allow the girl into the school in the first place was a mystery. She was obviously far too young and quite the most precocious brat Ophelia had ever come across. Once they were here, though, they were awfully hard to get rid of.

Ophelia grimaced as a painful memory invaded her thoughts. Another child, so like this one, a child to love, so adorable but . . . It was too hard to think about. Her feelings had almost destroyed her. She couldn't allow it. She wouldn't allow it. This child had to go, no matter the cost.

She suddenly remembered the new hardware she'd had installed during the break. Higgins was becoming more and more unreliable. Sappy love-struck girl—one day she would learn that there was more to life than love. Ophelia got out of bed and marched to her walk-in closet. She reached up and pressed the top button of her favorite vermilion Chanel suit. The rear wall slid apart to reveal a room, not large by any standards, but heaving under the weight of twenty-four video screens. Why she hadn't thought to do this sooner she really couldn't understand.

Chapter 18

When at last Alice-Miranda had drifted off to sleep she too had dreamt. About girls playing and laughing. The clanging of the school bell and a hundred pairs of feet running to their classrooms. It was a wonderful sleep, and when she awoke her stomach was aflurry with tiny butterflies. Alice-Miranda couldn't remember being this excited before.

"Good morning, Millie." She sat up in bed, clutching Brummel Bear to her chest.

"Oh, hello, Alice-Miranda." Millie opened her eyes sleepily, yawned and stretched her arms above her head. "Thanks for waking me. I hate that awful bell."

Just at that moment there was a loud clanging

noise accompanied by a shrill "Rise and shine, ladies, time to get up, time to sparkle, chop-chop, choppy-chop."

"Who is that?" Alice-Miranda asked.

"That's just Howie. You'll get used to it. She uses the same wake-up call every morning," Millie giggled.

"Howie?"

"Well, she's really Mrs. Howard but she's so used to Howie I don't think anyone has used her proper name in years." Millie swung her feet to the floor and scooped her slippers from beside the bed. "You'd better hurry up. If you don't get to the showers early you'll miss out on the hot water."

Alice-Miranda hopped up and pulled the sheets toward the bedhead.

"What are you doing?" Millie asked.

"Making the bed," Alice-Miranda replied as she carefully folded the sheets down over the top of the duvet and arranged the pillows.

"You know we don't have to. Howie always comes around and does them after we've gone to class." Millie dangled her toothbrush from her mouth as she donned a floral shower cap.

"Why should she have to do it?" Alice-Miranda smoothed the duvet and carefully rested Brummel Bear in the middle of her pillow.

"We're supposed to make them ourselves but we're all so terrible at it that she remakes them anyway. Alethea called a house meeting last year and said that no one had to make their beds because Howie would do it for us," Millie replied.

"That's not very fair. I'm sure she has more important things to do than make our beds." Alice-Miranda scrunched her feet into her slippers.

At that very moment Howie appeared at the doorway. Her frame took up almost the whole space.

"Good morning, girls. Hello, Millicent, did you have a good break, my dear?"

"Yes, Howie. And you?" Millie replied.

"Lovely. I spent a lot of time in the garden but rather more in the kitchen"—she patted her tummy—"if you know what I mean. And you must be one of our new poppets. It's Alice-Miranda, isn't it?"

"Yes, Mrs. Howard. Pleased to meet you." Alice-Miranda moved toward her and held out her hand. Mrs. Howard looked a little surprised but squeezed it gently.

"I'm sorry I wasn't here when you arrived, my sweet. Not like me at all, but there was trouble afoot with my youngest grandchild—she had the croup and I just couldn't leave until I knew she was going to be all right. That daughter of mine has quite the brood—seven and another on the way." Mrs. Howard's smile sent deep wrinkles to the corners of her eyes. She looked around the room and spied Alice-Miranda's freshly made bed.

"Darling girl. Did you do that?" Howie looked genuinely shocked as she inspected Alice-Miranda's handiwork.

"Yes, Mrs. Howard," Alice-Miranda replied. "I'm sorry if it's not quite right but my granny taught me to make my bed at home when I was six. She said that everyone should know how to make a bed and, well, seeing as though she'd once been a nurse, a long time ago in the war, she taught me how to do hospital corners. If you'd rather teach me your way, I'm very happy to learn." Alice-Miranda stood like a statue beside the perfectly made bed.

"Oh, no, my dear, it's wonderful. Perhaps you can teach the other girls?" She smiled widely and raised her eyebrows. "I'm sure Alethea would love some lessons."

Millie stuck her bottom lip out as far as she could manage.

"Yes, Millicent—I'm sure that's what Alethea would do, too. Now run along to the shower, girls. I'll lay your uniforms out on the beds before you come back." Howie bustled along the hallway clanging her bell.

Chapter 19

After breakfast, which consisted of the most delicious scrambled eggs, tea and toast, Millie took Alice-Miranda to the Great Hall, where the girls were to meet for assembly. When at last the bell rang to signify the start of term, Alice-Miranda wriggled in her seat. She craned her neck to see the teachers as they marched side by side down the center aisle, dressed in spectacular gowns with a rainbow of colored hoods. The new girls, of whom she was the very youngest, sat in the back rows while the older forms sat in front. The organist, who Millie had said was called Mr. Trout, waved his arms flamboyantly as he played a very complicated piece. He taught music, of course.

Alice-Miranda was yet to meet most of the staff but she recognized Miss Reedy and Mr. Plumpton, who stood at the end of the line. Mr. Plumpton's red nose glowed and he had to take two little running steps for every one of Miss Reedy's, but somehow he managed to look dignified just the same.

The teachers took their places on the stage and Miss Reedy stepped forward to speak.

"Good morning, girls, and welcome back for another year at Winchesterfield-Downsfordvale. I trust that you have all had a good holiday and are ready to give of your best. If not, you will find yourself spending a lot of time in detention with me. If you are new, I hope you are settling in well. You have all received a copy of the school rules—I suggest you read them closely and abide by them at all times. I have several announcements." A soft buzz echoed around the hall at this.

"She's going to announce the Head Prefect," Millie whispered, turning to Alice-Miranda, who was sitting in the row behind.

Miss Reedy was holding a large scroll. She adjusted her silver-framed glasses and let the scroll unfurl to the floor.

"Item number one. The new Head Prefect is . . ." Miss Reedy flinched.

"Oh no, it must be . . ." Millie winced, waiting for the inevitable. There was a much longer than necessary pause as Miss Reedy seemed unable to say the words. Finally she whispered, "Alethea Goldsworthy," and smiled thinly.

Alethea squealed from the front of the hall. "It's me, it's me!"

"Alethea, please come up and accept your badge." Miss Reedy looked around at Mr. Plumpton, who rolled his eyes.

Alethea ran to the side of the stage, bounded up the steps and snatched the badge from Miss Reedy's hand. She then shoved the teacher rather energetically from the lectern. She began her acceptance speech with another squeal.

"Girls, teachers, you have made a wonderful choice in me. I will be the best Head Prefect Winchesterfield-Downsfordvale has ever seen. Of course, there really was no other option." She smiled condescendingly along the row of girls from the Sixth Form.

Miss Reedy moved in beside Alethea and leaned into the microphone.

"Thank you, Alethea. Your graciousness and humility will no doubt be a highlight of the year."

A snicker of laughter rose up before Alethea shot a stare that would freeze fire.

"You may return to your seat, Alethea," Miss Reedy instructed.

"But I sit on the stage next to you now, Miss Reedy." Alethea's cat-with-the-cream smile was plastered all over her smug face.

"And so you do." Miss Reedy motioned toward the empty seat beside her own.

"Now we have to spend every assembly looking at that," Millie whispered.

Alice-Miranda leaned forward in her seat. "If she's really so terrible why did Miss Grimm allow it?"

"Remember the library." Millie didn't smile. "As long as your parents can pay, you can be whatever you want at Winchesterfield-Downsfordvale."

"That's awful," Alice-Miranda sighed. "Surely it hasn't always been like this? Mummy would have told me, and she has only ever said that it was a wonderful school."

"Legend has it that about ten years ago something terrible happened. The whole place changed, and since then, well, it seems as though the family that pays the most gets the most." Millie picked nervously at her fingernails.

Alice-Miranda caught sight of Miss Higgins standing just offstage. She looked pale and was wringing her hands together.

"Something's missing, Millie. Miss Grimm should be here. She's the headmistress and she should be leading the assembly."

"Tell *her* that," Millie whispered.

"Item number two," Miss Reedy's voice boomed. "All students under the age of eight will be required to sit an academic suitability test. If they are proven unsuitable the consequences may involve removal from the school."

A murmur shot around the room. The look of surprise on Miss Reedy's face suggested she was reading the rule for the very first time. She turned around to face the staff, who seemed equally shocked.

"That's a new one. I didn't have to sit any suitability test," Millie whispered.

"I didn't either. . . . Nor me . . . What's that all about?" the room buzzed.

"But there's nobody here who's under the age of eight," called Madeline Bloom, who had been silently doing her maths. "You're not supposed to come unless you've turned eight already."

"Well, I'm afraid there is someone," said Alice-Miranda, touching her left forefinger to her lips.

"Who?" asked Ivory Hicks.

"Me." Alice-Miranda smiled.

"Silence," Miss Reedy commanded. "Item number

three. Any girls under the age of eight must complete the Form Six Wilderness Walk: camping for five days in a tent, cooking her own food and navigating her own way through the forest. Failure to do so will render her unready for life at Winchesterfield-Downsfordvale." Miss Reedy gasped as she finished reading. "That's madness," she murmured under her breath, then gulped loudly when she realized that the microphone had picked up every word. She quickly moved on.

"Item number four." Miss Reedy took a deep breath, hardly daring to scan the page. She cleared her throat. "Item number four. Any student under the age of eight must challenge the school champion at a game of her choosing and win. If she fails in this endeavour she will be asked to leave the school, as she is clearly not ready to take on the challenges of life at Winchesterfield-Downsfordvale."

The whole hall erupted.

"That's so unfair. . . . No one's ever had to do that before. . . ."

"That's because we've never had any upstart seven-year-olds before," Alethea said loudly.

"Yes we have," Jacinta Headlington-Bear called back. "I started when I was only just seven."

"That's because your parents couldn't wait to be rid

of you," Alethea snapped from her position on the stage.

"Who made those rules, anyway?" Ashima asked Susannah, who was sitting in the row ahead of her.

"I did!" a voice boomed.

The girls searched the hall for the owner but couldn't see anyone.

"Who said that?" The words escaped from Susannah's mouth before she had time to stop them.

"I said it." The voice echoed through the hall. The teachers onstage sat in terrified silence.

"It's Miss Grimm," said Alice-Miranda. "I knew it wasn't true that she didn't come out of her study."

Alice-Miranda leapt to her feet, a beaming smile plastered on her face. "Hello, Miss Grimm. Where are you? I am so pleased that you're here. I mean, fancy having the first assembly of the year without the headmistress. Did you enjoy last night's supper? And did you sleep well? My stomach had so many butterflies it took me ages to settle down."

You could have heard a pin drop.

"Silence!" the voice demanded. "You will not speak in assembly, today or any other day, Alice-Miranda."

Alice-Miranda sat down softly. No one dared make a sound. A hundred mouths gaped open, waiting for the next instruction. Alice-Miranda leaned forward to whisper to Millie. Millie just shook her head, never once taking her eyes from the stage. Alice-Miranda closed her mouth and shuffled back in her seat.

There was a crackling of static and a collective realization that Miss Grimm was not in the hall at all.

"She's in there," Madeline whispered, pointing at the loudspeaker at the side of the stage.

"Close your mouths, girls," instructed the headmistress, her voice so sharp you could have cut your finger on it. "You are not fish."

"But how can she see us?" Jacinta Headlington-Bear giggled nervously.

"Miss Headlington-Bear, did I say something to amuse you?" Miss Grimm's voice scolded.

Jacinta reeled in shock, wondering how Miss Grimm even knew what she looked like.

"No, Miss Grimm," she mumbled, her eyes searching for a hole in the floor that might swallow her up.

"So I do not amuse you?" Miss Grimm continued.

"No, Miss Grimm," Jacinta said hesitantly.

"So I am not funny," Miss Grimm prodded.

"Yes, Miss Grimm." Jacinta closed her eyes and wished that she was anywhere but there.

"So you are saying that I am not funny and yet you choose to laugh at me." Miss Grimm was toying with Jacinta's nerves like a tabby with a field mouse.

"No, Miss Grimm." Jacinta gulped and tried to suppress the urge to be sick.

"Miss Headlington-Bear, what is it that you love more than anything in the world?"

"Gymnastics, Miss Grimm," Jacinta whispered.

"And the championships are next week, am I correct?" Miss Grimm asked.

"Yes, Miss Grimm." Jacinta's eyes welled with fat tears.

"And have you finished your assignment?"

"Yes, Miss Grimm."

Miss Grimm's voice softened. "I suppose you should be allowed to go, then."

"Oh, thank you, Miss Grimm." Jacinta beamed.

"Such a pity, then, that your rudeness *has just earned you the right not to go*." Miss Grimm's voice drilled into Jacinta.

"But Miss Grimm . . ." Jacinta began to sob.

"Stop that infernal noise," Miss Grimm commanded.

Alice-Miranda was about to speak when she felt a hand on her arm.

"Don't," Susannah mouthed.

Susannah was right. Perhaps it would be better to go and speak with Miss Grimm after the assembly. Poor Jacinta, it really wasn't fair, Alice-Miranda thought.

"You may continue with the assembly, Miss Reedy," Miss Grimm's voice boomed. "And make no mistake: there are no secrets in this school. I see everything. I hear everything." And with that, the crackle in the air ceased and Miss Grimm was gone.

The remainder of the assembly was very swift indeed.

Miss Reedy had stood like a statue during the entire exchange. She adjusted her glasses and stared out into the sea of anxious faces. She cleared her throat and ran her finger down the agenda.

"Yes, well, girls, as it is the first day of term we have no awards to hand out. We'll save our birthday wishes until teatime. No notices." Miss Reedy glanced quickly around at the staff seated behind her. Nobody moved. It was as though the voice from beyond had frozen them all to the spot.

"All right then, girls, it's off to first classes. The lists have been posted on the notice board outside. Well . . . a good term . . . yes . . ." She tried to smile but the girls were still too stunned to return the gesture.

Chapter 20

The girls left the assembly hall in silence. It was the first time Miss Reedy could remember not having to ask them to hold their chatter until they got outside. It was only as the girls spilled into the bright sunshine that they regained the use of their tongues.

"What was all that?" Millie grabbed Alice-Miranda's arm and guided her toward the notice boards.

"What have you done to Miss Grimm, Alice-Miranda?" asked Madeline as she caught up. "All those rules and they only apply to you."

"I can't imagine." Alice-Miranda smiled. "But it's

all right. Miss Grimm wants me to prove I deserve to be here, so that's what I'll do."

Millie shook her head. "But all those things you have to do. I don't think many of us could manage them. I hate camping. All those bugs and things. Ick!"

"I don't mind." Alice-Miranda was eager to find out about her lessons. She ran her finger down the list to see where her first class was. To her great delight she was going to English and her teacher was Miss Reedy. She wasn't about to let Miss Grimm's new rules upset her. Goodness, there were far more important things to think about. At least Miss Reedy was still teaching English, even if it was to the youngest girls rather than the senior classes. Alice-Miranda was looking forward to meeting her.

Just as she was about to look for her classroom, a shadow fell across her face. Alethea stepped into her path, her three followers lined up behind her. Alethea's shiny Head Prefect badge glinted in the sunlight, the newest trophy to adorn her royal blue blazer.

"There you are, little girl. Didn't I tell you yesterday that you have to do everything I say? And now I have the badge to prove it." Alethea smiled, her thin lips curling smugly. "When will you be delivering that special mineral water, *from Switzerland?*" she mimicked. "I think I might like some right about . . . NOW!"

"Oh, hello, Alethea. Congratulations, what a lovely honor. Perhaps I might get to be Head Prefect one day. I'd love it, you know, but Mummy says that with privilege comes responsibility. So I suppose that really means you have to be the most responsible girl in the whole school. That's big, isn't it?" asked Alice-Miranda. "Of course you can have my mineral water—I wouldn't have offered it if I didn't mean for you to have it, but I will have to bring it to you after lessons."

Alethea crossed her arms and blocked Alice-Miranda's path.

"I want it now!" Her eyebrows arched menacingly.

"She wants it now!" the three marionettes chorused from behind her.

"Alethea, I *will* bring it to you. I promise. But I really must go to class. I would hate to be late on my first day." With this Alice-Miranda began to move off.

"Don't you walk away from me!" Alethea shouted. "You have to do everything *I* say and *I* say *go and get my mineral water*." Alethea's face resembled an angry bulldog's.

The courtyard, which had been buzzing with girls' chatter, was suddenly silent.

"Leave her alone," said Millie, and grabbed Alice-Miranda's arm to lead her away.

"Who are you again? Oh, that's right—it's the freckle-faced freak from the farm." Alethea's words sliced through the air like a warm knife through a slab of butter.

"Alethea, that was awfully unkind. Millie is just trying to help. There's no need to call her names." Alice-Miranda moved closer to Alethea. Everyone else reeled backward, not daring to imagine what might happen next.

"GET ME MY MINERAL WATER!" Alethea leaned forward and screamed into Alice-Miranda's face. Her blond hair was standing on end and Alice-Miranda could almost see sparks zapping from her tongue.

Miss Higgins, who had been on her way to see Mrs. Oliver about the luncheon menu, heard the noise and stopped in her tracks. "Oh dear, this is going to be bad, very bad." She had seen it all too many times before. She ran on her high heels to where the girls were frozen to the spot.

"There you are, Alice-Miranda." She swiftly put herself between the two girls. "You need to come with me."

And with that Miss Higgins grabbed Alice-Miranda's tiny hand and wrenched her from the heart of danger.

When they were safely out of sight, Miss Higgins

stopped and turned to Alice-Miranda. She crouched down, her blue eyes meeting Alice-Miranda's brown saucers.

"Sweetheart, you really mustn't upset Alethea—especially now that she's Head Girl." Miss Higgins pushed a stray curl behind Alice-Miranda's ear.

"It's all right, Miss Higgins. I'm not afraid of her. I promised her my mineral water and she just asked for it."

Without warning, Alice-Miranda leaned forward and gave Miss Higgins a hug.

Miss Higgins smiled in surprise. "Oh, what's that for?"

"Because everyone needs a hug sometimes," Alice-Miranda said, and smiled back.

"Well, off you go to class. You don't want to keep Miss Reedy waiting." Miss Higgins straightened Alice-Miranda's blazer.

"How did you know that I have English with Miss Reedy?"

"I told you I have a very important job to do. One of the tasks is keeping a close eye on you girls." Miss Higgins stood up. "What about if I walk you to class? I can show you exactly where the room is." She wanted to see Alice-Miranda safely out of Alethea's way, at least for the next couple of hours.

"That's very kind, Miss Higgins, but you really don't have to. I'm sure it's not hard to find and I know you have a thousand other more important things to be doing," said Alice-Miranda. She checked her pigtails and retied one of her ribbons.

"It's no bother at all. I was on my way to see Mrs. Oliver. She is a darling woman and a jolly good cook too. Your classroom is on the way, just over there." Miss Higgins pointed.

Alice-Miranda looked up. "Well, if it's really no bother. Thank you." She held Miss Higgins's hand and they walked together across the courtyard.

Meanwhile, in the depths of her wardrobe, Ophelia Grimm was monitoring the screens. Although she had cameras concealed in various locations, only some were connected to pick up sound. She had watched the angry scene between Alice-Miranda and Alethea. No doubt the little brat had broken some school rule and needed to be chastised. Yes, she thought, Alethea was an excellent choice for Head Prefect.

It was fortunate for Alice-Miranda that Miss Grimm had been called away to the bathroom when Miss Higgins received her hug. Goodness only knows what kind of trouble there might have been for both of them if Miss Grimm had seen such outrageous affection.

Chapter 21

By the end of her first week, Alice-Miranda was tired but truly happy. Her teachers were very clever and the lessons were so much more interesting than at her old school, where she always felt a bit like the nanny in the nursery. The children at Ellery Prep were fun and she had loads of lovely friends but they all seemed so young. Winchesterfield-Downsfordvale couldn't have suited her any better. She especially loved her English lessons with Miss Reedy, who knew more about books than anyone Alice-Miranda had ever met.

Alice-Miranda called her parents once each day and was always greeted with, "Oh, darling, so it really is awful? We'll come and get you straight away." To which she would tell them that she was having the most wonderful time and they should stop worrying. She often thought that for grown-ups, they could be very hard to manage.

With Millie's help she had delivered the mineral water and it seemed that for now Alethea was happy to leave her alone. Perhaps that was because Miss Higgins had decided that the best way to keep Alethea away from Alice-Miranda was to give Alethea as many duties as she could possibly find. Never mind that she spent her entire life moaning and complaining that what was the use of being Head Prefect if you had to do all of the work? She didn't do it anyway; she just passed her jobs to Lizzy, Danika and Shelby, who for the moment felt very powerful and important by virtue of being Alethea's best friends.

Mrs. Oliver's first full week had been a cracking success. The girls devoured their dinners and often went back for more. Miss Higgins thought that perhaps when Mrs. Smith returned, Mrs. Oliver might stay on for another week to teach her some new recipes—if that was all right with Alice-Miranda's parents, of course.

Mr. Charles was having a wonderful time in the

garden working alongside Mr. Greening and his men. The two of them had spent almost a whole day planning the color schemes and layouts. Mr. Charles was still scared stiff that it might cost him his job, but the joy of having flowers back at Winchesterfield-Downsfordvale made it all worthwhile.

Every afternoon at four p.m. Alice-Miranda would stop into the greenhouse and Mr. Charles would give her a full update on what had been planted where, and when the flowers would bloom. She would make him a cup of tea and bring over a little napkin filled with whatever delicious treat Mrs. Oliver had given her from the kitchen. There was tea bun and vanilla slice and one day she surprised him with a huge piece of chocolate cake.

"Where did that come from?" he marveled as she unwrapped the sticky treasure.

"It's Ivory's birthday today, so Mrs. Oliver baked her the most delicious chocolate cake with cream frosting. You should have seen the look on Alethea's face when she saw it. She immediately said that for her birthday next month she demanded a cake twice the size and it had to be decorated entirely with chocolate sprinkles." Alice-Miranda giggled when she told him.

"She's a greedy one, that Alethea." Charlie shovelled the gooey confection into his mouth.

Alice-Miranda laughed when she saw him.

He realized what she was laughing at. "And I'm a one to talk." He smiled as he licked his fingers, making sure there was not one crumb wasted.

Alice-Miranda's strange feeling had all but disappeared in the past week. The only time it niggled was when she thought about Miss Grimm, sitting alone in her study. She tried not to let it bother her but she couldn't help wondering what it was that kept the headmistress so busy all the time. She had tried to see her several times during the week, particularly to ask if she might change her mind about Jacinta and the championships. But each time she went to the office, Miss Higgins insisted that Miss Grimm was too busy. She wrote a letter and left it with Miss Higgins but didn't hear a thing.

Alice-Miranda felt terrible for Jacinta and went to talk to her. Jacinta's face was puffy from crying but she thanked Alice-Miranda for trying and said that she would keep up her training just in case she might be allowed to go at the last minute.

By the end of the week Alice-Miranda understood a little better about Miss Grimm's being busy. Her own days were full to the brim and she always went to bed exhausted.

During the week, Miss Grimm had watched carefully

as life moved on around her. That impudent child didn't seem to be causing any real trouble, but she had wondered what all the fuss was in the grounds— trucks coming and going and men all over the place.

It was fortunate for Charlie that they were planting seedlings and bulbs, which weren't yet visible in the gardens. When Miss Grimm asked Miss Higgins what was going on out there, she was told that Charlie was having some help laying out new irrigation. Miss Higgins hated lying but there was nothing to be gained in upsetting Miss Grimm. Far better to let the flowers speak for themselves in a few months' time. Anyway, Miss Higgins thought, by the time the flowers bloomed, she would be married. And in all likelihood the teachers and girls at Winchesterfield-Downsfordvale would have to look after themselves.

And then there was the business of Alice-Miranda's academic suitability test. Miss Grimm decided that she alone would set the test. It would have to be done on the Monday of the second week of term. Better not to let the little terror become too attached to her new surroundings.

Chapter 22

"When do you have to take that wretched test?" Millie asked, looking up from her poetry books. Alice-Miranda was busily studying long division.

"I don't know, really. I suppose Miss Grimm will decide. Perhaps I should go over and ask her?"

"I think you should stay right away from her. She wasn't exactly pleased to see you last Sunday. Maybe that's why she decided that you have to do all those horrid things." Millie ruled a line in thick red pen under her heading. "It's so unfair. I mean, she hasn't even told you what's going to be in the test. What if it's something really hard that you've never even heard of before?"

"I'll just do my best. That's all she can ask of me. She knows I'm only seven and one-quarter and I've only had seven and one-quarter years to learn whatever it is that I've learned." Alice-Miranda finished her calculations and moved on to her grammar homework.

Millie smiled to herself. For someone who had only been around for seven and one-quarter years, Alice-Miranda seemed so much older. Millie had never met anyone like her. Usually she would have complained loudly about being stuck in a room with one of the youngest girls—especially now that she had been at Winchesterfield-Downsfordvale for over two years—but there was something about Alice-Miranda that was hard to resist.

"Hello, little girls." A snarly voice floated through the open doorway, followed by its equally vicious owner.

"Hello, Alethea," said Alice-Miranda, looking up.

"Hello, Alethea," Millie echoed less enthusiastically.

Alethea walked into the room and immediately plonked onto Alice-Miranda's bed. She snatched up Brummel Bear and pinched his nose.

Alice-Miranda glanced around and then continued

with her homework. "That's Brummel Bear. He's very pleased to meet you."

"You're such a baby." Alethea threw the bear back onto the bed and laughed in disgust. "Are these your parents?" She picked up a silver-framed photograph from a pair on Alice-Miranda's bedside table.

"Yes, that's Mummy." Alice-Miranda stopped what she was doing and walked over to Alethea. She picked up the other frame and showed it to her. "And that's my darling daddy."

"I've seen them before somewhere. Are they famous? My daddy's famous. He owns an oil company. But I suppose you knew that already." It wasn't really a question.

"Really? Good on him. That must be very exciting. I imagine he flies all over the world visiting different countries and giving jobs to thousands of very poor people," Alice-Miranda replied.

"More like stealing from third-world countries and making people work for next to nothing in the most hideous circumstances," Millie said under her breath. A recent geography lesson on oil drilling had left her with no false impressions about exactly how Addison Goldsworthy had made his fortune.

"What was that, Freckles?" Alethea's tongue flicked like an asp's.

"Nothing, Alethea. I was just thinking how lovely it must be to have a daddy who can buy you everything you would ever want." Millie rolled her eyes, keeping her head firmly in her books.

"Yes, it is wonderful. I mean, I wouldn't know what it's like to be poor. Fancy having to be here on a"— Alethea gulped as though the words were stuck in the back of her throat—"a scholarship."

"Well, I think it's wonderful that we have girls here on scholarships," Alice-Miranda replied. "Winchesterfield-Downsfordvale has so many things to offer—it would be terrible if you could only come here because your parents were rich."

"You have a lot to learn, little one." Alethea pulled Alice-Miranda's ponytail.

"Ow," Alice-Miranda couldn't help squealing.

Millie looked around, wondering about Alethea's next move. This wasn't a social visit. Alethea's visits never were. Alethea had something on her mind and Millie feared that they were about to find out what it was.

"Did you enjoy your mineral water?" Alice-Miranda asked innocently.

"It was horrid, actually. Don't know how you drink the stuff." That seemed to remind Alethea about the reason for her visit. "So, I've decided that tomorrow morning you're going to wash my hair with it instead. Then you're going to wash Lizzy's and Danika's and even Shelby's nasty mop. By the way, I think she has lice, but I'm sure that you'll manage to comb them out first." Alethea smiled thinly.

Millie protested. "You can't make Alice-Miranda wash your hair. That's disgraceful. Howie will have something to say about that."

Alethea lay back onto Alice-Miranda's bed.

"Howie is off this weekend. It's her son's wedding or some other vile family event. Shaker's on, so, my dear little girls, this weekend you are both mine." Alethea twisted a strand of blond hair menacingly around her forefinger much the same way she planned to twist Alice-Miranda and Millie.

Millie looked crushed.

Alethea jumped up off the bed and turned on her heel.

"See you tomorrow, little slaves," she said, and flounced down the corridor.

"That's gross," Millie sighed. "I don't want to touch her hair."

"It could be worse," said Alice-Miranda. "So who's Shaker?"

"She comes when Howie's not here, which thankfully is hardly ever. She's about ninety and she's as

{127}

deaf as a beetle and her eyesight is failing too. She thinks Alethea is a darling and now that Alethea is Head Prefect it will only be worse. There's no use complaining to her because she really wouldn't know what to do anyway."

"Surely it's not that bad." Alice-Miranda tried to sound positive. She began to laugh. "Anyway, Alethea might regret that decision."

"What do you mean?" Millie looked puzzled.

"Well, my mineral water from Switzerland is delicious. But it's not very good at all for washing hair. When I went with Mummy and Daddy to visit their old friend the baron last year, Mummy commented how simply splendid it would be to have water as beautiful as this to wash her hair in. The baroness did not agree. Apparently she had tried it and found that the water was far too hard. Her hair lost all its shine for a month. It was terribly dull and flat," Alice-Miranda explained. "I really should warn Alethea."

Millie giggled. "No, that's perfect. Alethea needs to learn that she has no right at all to order you about. She loves her hair. She spends half the day preening those delicious blond locks. If it means that she's about to go from golden-haired Barbie to flat and dull Bertha, I won't mind one bit."

Chapter 23

On Saturday morning at breakfast Miss Reedy made her usual round of announcements. She directed girls to their various games and read a list of activities that were available over the weekend. But it was her final point that caused a buzz.

"Alice-Miranda Highton-Smith-Kennington-Jones, you must go immediately after breakfast to see Miss Higgins." She peered over her glasses at Alice-Miranda from the dining room lectern.

The room was suddenly alive with gossip. The usual staccato chinking of spoons on bowls and light thuds as cups were set back down on tables was over-run by loudly whispered speculation.

"She's getting kicked out already," Lizzy gloated.

"No, she probably has to do that test." Danika leaned her head forward around Alethea to meet Lizzy's gaze.

"She'd better not be going today. It's hair-washing day," Alethea hissed, loudly enough to be heard by the girls sitting with Alice-Miranda at the next table.

"Oh, she's so awful," Ashima whispered, and shook her head. "Don't worry, Alice-Miranda, it's probably nothing at all." She crossed her fingers under the table.

"It's all right. I'm not worried. Perhaps Miss Grimm wants to talk to me about my letter. I wrote to her earlier in the week to ask if she would reconsider her decision about Jacinta and the championships. It's probably that." Alice-Miranda went back to munching daintily on her cornflakes.

"I'll have to wash all that hair on my own," Millie groaned, pointing over her shoulder toward Alethea's table.

"No you won't," Madeline chimed in. "The four of us agreed that we'd help. Then it will all be over in less than an hour and we can go off for some games."

Ashima, Ivory and Susannah nodded in agreement.

"You guys are the best," Millie said, and smiled.

"And don't worry, I'll be back soon," said Alice-

Miranda. She hopped up and gathered her dish and spoon. She deposited them on the food counter and asked Miss Reedy if she might be excused.

"Certainly, Alice-Miranda. And if it's about that test," she lowered her voice, "well, I'm rather hoping that you might have some time to study. Perhaps you would like to come and see me this afternoon and we can go over a few things?"

"That would be lovely, thank you, Miss Reedy." Alice-Miranda smiled. She couldn't believe some of the things the girls had said about her. Miss Reedy didn't seem the least bit like a fire-breathing dragon with a toothache.

Alice-Miranda left the dining room and started out across the flagstones.

"Morning, Miss Alice-Miranda," Charlie called from the other side of the courtyard. He tipped his hat and smiled.

"Good morning, Mr. Charles," she called back.

He grinned widely. There was something about that child, he thought, and smiled to himself, before picking up the arms of his wheelbarrow and trundling toward the greenhouse.

Alice-Miranda knocked loudly on the office door.

"Come in," Miss Higgins called.

"Hello, Miss Higgins." Alice-Miranda beamed. "Is

Miss Grimm in?" She looked toward the oak doors that led to the study.

"I'm afraid she's very busy this morning." Miss Higgins was flicking through some pages on her desk. "But she did ask me to give you this." She passed Alice-Miranda a large envelope with her name on the front.

"Oh, I hope she's changed her mind about Jacinta. Has she?" Alice-Miranda asked, clutching the envelope to her chest.

"Please don't get your hopes up, Alice-Miranda. I haven't known Miss Grimm to change her mind— about anything, really." Miss Higgins looked doleful.

Alice-Miranda carefully opened the envelope. It held a very official-looking letter on the school letterhead.

WINCHESTERFIELD–DOWNSFORDVALE ACADEMY FOR PROPER YOUNG LADIES

Dear Miss Highton-Smith-Kennington-
   Jones,

   As you are aware, a list of school
   regulations was read out in the
   morning assembly on Monday. It would

appear that these new rules apply to you, as you are seven and one-quarter years old. I have outlined the following schedule for you to undertake the activities discussed.

1. **WEEK TWO: Monday**
   Three-hour academic test

2. **WEEK THREE: Monday-Friday**
   Wilderness Walk: a 20-kilometer hike over five days

3. **WEEK FOUR: Friday**
   Sporting competition in a game of your selection against the current school champion

Each of these tests requires your utmost attention. Whether you pass or fail will be wholly at my discretion, although you should take the following as a guide. Your mark for the academic test will be not less than 95%. You must complete the

Wilderness Walk without any
assistance and survive, and you
must win the sporting competition.
Failure to complete any or all of
the above will result in your being
asked to leave the school. Given
that any return may be distressing
for the other girls, there would be
no place for you, even when you have
turned eight.

  May I suggest that the remainder
of your weekend be spent studying a
range of subjects, including English
literature, mathematics, science,
history and geography. Although I
will not guarantee that the test
will include any of the above.

Yours sincerely,

Miss Ophelia Grimm
Headmistress

P.S.: In response to your letter
regarding Jacinta Headlington-Bear,
the answer is no, she may not attend

{134}

the championships. There will be no
further discussion of the matter.
Her parents are well aware of her
totally unacceptable and insolent
behavior and support my decision
without reservation.

Alice-Miranda's shoulders slumped. "But that's so unfair." She put the letter on the edge of Miss Higgins's desk.

"I gather it's not good news." Miss Higgins looked at the piece of paper.

"Go on; please read it for yourself, Miss Higgins," sighed Alice-Miranda. "I don't mind at all about the first part. If I have to prove that I belong here then I know I can do that. It's the last part. It's so awful. Poor Jacinta will be heartbroken. Do you know how good she is? I've seen some pretty fantastic gymnasts but she's amazing."

"Well, you did your best, Alice-Miranda. You tried and that's more than any of the other girls would do for Jacinta. She's not exactly the easiest person to get along with." Miss Higgins gently touched Alice-Miranda's cheek.

"I know. Goodness, when I met her last weekend she was having the most fabulous tantrum. But when she calmed down, you know, she was really quite reasonable. I think she's lonely. Her parents didn't even take her home for the holidays. I can't imagine Mummy and Daddy not coming to pick me up—no matter how busy they are."

"I suppose her life is rather complicated," Miss Higgins replied. She stared at the papers on her desk, deep in thought, then looked up and smiled. "However did you get to be so wise, young lady?"

Chapter 24

Alice-Miranda glanced at the grandfather clock in the corner of Miss Higgins's office.

"Goodness, it's already after nine!" She folded the letter and returned it to its envelope. "I need to get back to the house and help poor Millie with Alethea's hair."

"You need to do what?" Miss Higgins's eyes widened.

"It's a long story, Miss Higgins, and I'm sure you don't have time for it now. I should go, otherwise poor Millie and the other girls will have to do all the work without me. Considering it was my mineral water that caused the problem in the first place, that would be awfully unfair." Alice-Miranda walked toward the door. "Perhaps before I go back I should find poor Jacinta and tell her that Miss Grimm hasn't changed her mind." Alice-Miranda tapped her finger on the envelope. "It's just that I hate to disappoint her."

"No, Alice-Miranda, don't do that just yet. I have another idea. Jacinta's parents are awfully well off. Perhaps if I suggest to Miss Grimm a donation of some sort, she might just reconsider." Miss Higgins rested her chin in her hands.

"So Millie was right." Alice-Miranda sighed and placed her hands on her hips.

"About what?" Miss Higgins asked.

"Well, Millie said that the only reason Alethea is Head Prefect is that her father paid an enormous amount of money to build the new library. She said whoever pays the most gets the most. I think that's just awful. What about the girls who are here on scholarship? Their parents could never afford to pay extra. I'm sure they struggle just to manage the uniforms and things. My mummy came here and my grandmother and all my aunts and they have only ever said that this was the most wonderful school, with so much . . . what's the word I'm looking for . . . it starts with i, I think . . ." Alice-Miranda's voice trailed off.

"*Integrity*. That's the word you're looking for." Miss Higgins looked ashamed. "I'm sorry for suggesting it, Alice-Miranda. It's just that in the last ten years, Miss Grimm . . . Well, things have changed and I couldn't say for the better. I shouldn't be telling you this; in fact, I can't understand why I am even thinking about telling you. You're a child and you don't need to be thrown headlong into the awful world of grown-ups." Miss Higgins's eyes glazed over and Alice-Miranda thought she was about to cry.

"What is it, Miss Higgins? What happened to Miss Grimm?" urged Alice-Miranda.

"I can't." Miss Higgins turned away, then stood and walked to the filing cabinet behind her. Hurriedly she pulled open the top drawer and began flicking through the files. Without looking up from her task she said, "Off you go, Alice-Miranda. Please don't say anything to Jacinta. I will see if Miss Grimm will change her mind, and I won't mention anything about a donation. But you should go and see Miss Reedy. She'll help you study for the test. Please work hard. It would be so terrible . . ." Her voice quavered.

"What would be terrible, Miss Higgins?" Alice-Miranda was standing in the doorway holding the envelope rigidly.

"To lose you," Miss Higgins whispered, and motioned with her hand for Alice-Miranda to go.

Only when she heard the door click shut did Miss Higgins dare to look up. Two fat tears tumbled from her eyes, splashing onto Alice-Miranda's file. They couldn't lose her—Winchesterfield-Downsfordvale needed a girl like Alice-Miranda now more than ever.

Chapter 25

The hair washing went mostly without incident. Alice-Miranda arrived just in time to do Alethea's hair herself. Alethea had spent the first half-hour bossing Millie and the other girls about, telling them exactly how she thought things should be done. The fact that the whole exercise had to take place in the dormitory bathroom added somewhat to the drama. Alethea decided that she must have a proper salon with chairs and basins. The hand basins would do, but she sent Shelby and Lizzy to see Charlie. They demanded that he come to the house and set up a row of chairs at exactly the right height so the girls could lean their heads back into the sinks, like in a real salon. But they had to be comfortable, which any person who's ever sat in one of those salon chairs knows is almost impossible. The only thing that makes having your neck angled at ninety degrees even bearable is the thought of the delicious head massage. So after considerable stamping of feet and screeching from Alethea, Charlie somehow managed to angle the chairs toward the basin at what seemed to be the right height.

"Alethea, lean back, please," Alice-Miranda begged. She was standing on a footstool that Charlie had found for her. "I can't reach if you keep on leaning forward and you'll end up with water all down your back."

"But it hurts," Alethea complained. "Hurry up and get on with it. And you'd better do a good job—or perhaps you'd like to do this every Saturday morning for practice?" she snapped.

"I'd rather wash Charlie's gardening socks," Millie sighed under her breath.

"That could be arranged," Alethea replied. Millie flinched when she realized Alethea had heard her.

A pile of empty mineral-water bottles littered the tiled floor.

"What a waste," Madeline whispered as she began picking them up and depositing them into a large garbage bag, which Charlie had brought up earlier. He had sensed that there was something not quite right about the situation but knew well enough that if it involved Miss Goldsworthy it was far better left alone. Besides, Alice-Miranda had an army of assistants and if anyone could handle a tricky situation it was that little one.

Alice-Miranda found that running a comb through Alethea's blond locks was more difficult than she had expected. The mineral water seemed to strip the conditioner away, leaving a tangled mess.

"Ow, ow, ow!" Alethea squealed. "You're hurting me!" She grabbed Alice-Miranda's arm and began to inflict a very nasty Chinese burn.

"Stop it, Alethea!" Alice-Miranda commanded. "Now you're hurting me."

Alethea withdrew her hands immediately, startled at being told off.

"You wanted me to do your hair and I am doing my very best. There are a few knots and I am trying to untangle them. So if you don't mind, please be quiet and enjoy having your hair done," Alice-Miranda demanded.

The other girls were horrified. They had never heard Alice-Miranda raise her voice before, let alone dare to speak to Alethea in such a way.

"Oh no," Ashima whispered to Ivory. "We're going to get it now."

But to everyone's surprise Alice-Miranda managed to get the rest of the tangles out without much more than a yelp here and there. When at last she was finished, Alethea spent at least fifteen minutes admiring her reflection in the mirror. Fortunately she hadn't realized that her hair looked a lot less shiny than before they washed it.

"Beautiful," Alethea sighed.

"It must be hard to be you," said Millie. She stood behind Alethea, smiling at her in the mirror.

"Whatever do you mean?" Alethea flicked her hair over her shoulder. "I should think it's very easy being me. I'm rich, I'm beautiful and I can do anything I want. Silly girl, being me is a dream."

Millie turned away and put two fingers in her mouth. She spun back around to face Alethea, who had at last managed to drag herself away from her reflection.

"Of course. I only meant that, well, there's such pressure to be beautiful today. And goodness, beauty does take time," Millie said with a smile.

"That's not something you'll ever have to worry about, Freckles, is it, now?" With that Alethea strode out of the bathroom, leaving Alice-Miranda, Millie and the other girls surveying the puddles of water.

"She's foul," Madeline said with a shake of her head. "Don't let her worry you, Millie."

"I wonder why she feels the need to be nasty?" Alice-Miranda asked as she picked up a cloth and began wiping down the first sink. "Perhaps her mother isn't very nice to her."

"She's just spoiled rotten," Susannah replied. "But we've only got to cope with her for another year and then she'll be gone. Thank goodness Winchesterfield-Downsfordvale is a prep school. Imagine putting up with her all the way to leaving."

"Where is she going next?" Alice-Miranda looked up from her scrubbing.

"I don't know and I don't care," Millie replied. "Although I suppose we'd better find out and make sure that none of us is going there too. Imagine—having a couple of years off and then suddenly arriving at the new school only to find . . . Alethea." Millie called the name like a narrator in a horror movie, then clutched her hands to her throat and stuck her tongue out.

"Come on, let's get this place cleaned up." Ashima picked up the towels draped over the chairs.

"Can you help me take the chairs back to Charlie?" Alice-Miranda asked Millie.

"No—I'll go and get him and he can take them," she replied.

"But he's so busy in the garden. I'm sure we could manage." Alice-Miranda picked up a chair and began walking it out the door.

"Okay, I'm coming," Millie called, and followed her into the hall. "By the way, you didn't tell us what happened with Miss Higgins."

Alice-Miranda walked the chair slowly down the steps, careful not to tumble forward under its weight.

"It was nothing, really. Just an outline of when I have to do all those things Miss Reedy read out on Monday."

"Well, when do you have to do them?" Millie asked.

"I have to sit the test on Monday."

"Monday? That's so unfair! You don't even know what you have to study. Did she say what the pass mark would be?" Millie asked.

"Ninety-five percent. And I sort of know what I should be studying, so right after we finish cleaning up I'm going to see Miss Reedy. She offered to help me this morning." Alice-Miranda continued to the bottom of the steps with the chair.

"Gosh, that's amazing." Millie grinned. "Reedy actually offered to help you? She's usually too busy on the weekends with Mr. Plumpton. She must really like you, Alice-Miranda."

The two girls made their way over to the greenhouse,

{146}

where they found Charlie trimming his orchids. They left the chairs outside.

"What was all that, then?" he asked Alice-Miranda. "Did you do something to upset Miss Goldsworthy?"

"No, it was nothing." Alice-Miranda smiled. "Thanks for the chairs. I wasn't sure where they came from, so we've set them down outside. What's all that over there?" Alice-Miranda had spied a broken orchid and a crumpled blanket in the corner of the greenhouse.

"I don't know, miss," Charlie replied. "I came in this morning and found it like that."

Millie's eyes widened. "Maybe there's a tramp about. Imagine—someone lurking around the grounds at night. How exciting!" She shivered.

"Goodness, Miss Millie, that's quite an imagination you have there. I'm sure there's no one about these parts 'cept me and the other staff—and all you girls, of course." Charlie shook his head. "More likely some of the girls playing hide-and-seek."

Alice-Miranda studied the bedraggled pile. An uncomfortable thought occurred to her, but she shook it off quickly.

"I was just about to put the pot on. Can I interest you girls in a cup o' tea?" Charlie lit the stove.

"Sorry, Mr. Charles, I can't stay. I've got a test to study for—but Millie might like to join you."

"You're welcome to, lass." Charlie smiled at Millie. "I've got a lovely treat from Mrs. Oliver." He lifted a cloth to reveal an enormous piece of apple pie.

"Gosh," Alice-Miranda laughed. "You must be her favorite."

Millie hesitated. "Are you sure?" she asked Charlie.

"It'd be nice to have some company, Miss Millie." Charlie's blue eyes sparkled.

"See you later, Alice-Miranda—good luck with Miss Reedy," Millie said as she pulled up a chair.

Meanwhile, Ophelia Grimm was watching from her wardrobe. There were several cameras trained on the courtyard that Alice-Miranda had to cross before heading back to the dormitory.

Miss Grimm tracked Alice-Miranda as she skipped along, oblivious to the unseen eyes. "So, she doesn't need to study for my test," Miss Grimm said. "Thinks she can pass by flitting about, does she? We'll see about that."

Miss Grimm got up from her seat and slammed the secret door shut. It was time to set that test.

Chapter 26

Alice-Miranda spent the remainder of the afternoon and almost all of Sunday with her head in various books. True to her word, Miss Reedy sat with Alice-Miranda for hours, reading her written responses and setting quizzes. In all her years as a teacher she could not recall meeting another child with such a prodigious memory.

"What's the capital of Ethiopia?" she fired.

"Addis Ababa."

"Correct. How many wives did King Henry the Eighth have?"

"Six," Alice-Miranda shot back.

"Name them." Miss Reedy arched an eyebrow, quite sure that this would trip her up.

"That would be Catherine of Aragon, Anne Boleyn, Jane Seymour, Anne of Cleves, Catherine Howard and Catherine Parr."

"Is that the correct order?" Miss Reedy asked.

Alice-Miranda looked to the ceiling and counted them off on her fingers.

"Well, I'm sure that they are the right names. Mummy and Daddy took me to the Tower of London and I think I remember reading somewhere about Queen Catherine, who ended up divorced, and then I'm sure that it was Anne Boleyn who came next. Mummy says that she was terribly ambitious and look where that got her. Her head on the block." Alice-Miranda shuddered at the thought of it. "I'm fairly certain that the next wife was Jane and she died just after having a baby. Then I think it was Anne of Cleves, who he didn't find the least bit attractive. Poor girl—imagine going to another country to marry some revolting old man that you had never met and then he doesn't even like you. Very unfair. Anyway, he divorced her too, I think. Then came Catherine Howard, another silly girl—a cousin of Anne Boleyn. She ended up the same, with the axe. Last was Catherine Parr. The King died before

her. She was lucky, really, because he did have a terrible reputation for killing off his wives."

Alice-Miranda finally took a breath. Miss Reedy
stared at her with her mouth open.

"Good gracious, Alice-Miranda. You have given me
quite the potted royal history. However do you remember it all? I know girls twice your age who would
find learning all that very daunting." Miss Reedy
shook her head in disbelief.

"I don't know. I just remember things. I love visiting old places and thinking about all the people who
were there before me. When I was five Mummy and
Daddy took me to Rome. It was amazing to see all
those ancient places. I could have spent days in the
Colosseum—it was awful to think of all those poor
animals killed in the fights, and the people too. But
it was glamorous as well, with all the women and
their beautiful togas."

By teatime on Sunday Miss Reedy said that they
had done enough.

"Can we do one last quiz?" Alice-Miranda asked as
Miss Reedy stifled a yawn.

"My dear girl, you are exhausted and so am I," Miss
Reedy replied. "I suspect that Miss Grimm's test might
not trouble you much at all. Anyway, you can only do
your best. That's all anyone can ever ask of you."

"Thank you so much for helping me, Miss Reedy. I'm not really bothered about the test. I just don't want to disappoint anyone." Alice-Miranda closed her workbook and began packing her pencils.

Fortunately Miss Grimm's camera network did not extend into every room in the school. She had not seen Miss Reedy and Alice-Miranda working away throughout Saturday afternoon and almost all of Sunday. It most likely did not matter anyway. Ophelia Grimm typed furiously as she wrote the final question on the test: *How many wives did King Henry the Eighth have? Name them in order.*

"No child of seven and one-quarter will know the answer to that," Miss Grimm said to herself as she hit print. The pages whirred from the printer. She quickly snapped them up and reread the test from start to finish. There were a couple of questions that might challenge some of her staff members. An unpleasant thought began to invade her head. Perhaps she was being unduly harsh.

"Good grief, woman, stop it." Ophelia clutched her hands to her head. "She shouldn't be here. She's too young and she talks too much and . . . she's so like *her*." Miss Grimm stood up, determined to banish these ridiculous thoughts from her mind. She wouldn't allow herself to be hurt again. She stalked to the far end of the study and drew back the curtain. Charlie was weeding the garden bed in the middle of the drive. Was that whistling she could hear? Was he smiling? The man must be going mad. She would write a note immediately for Miss Higgins to deliver. Whistling was banned at Winchesterfield-Downsfordvale. What was he thinking, and why did he look so happy? Everyone knew that Charlie was a miserable old ox.

Chapter 27

Alice-Miranda was summoned to Miss Higgins's office during breakfast on Monday morning. Miss Reedy smiled at her when she made the announcement, then mouthed "Good luck" as Alice-Miranda walked by the teachers' table.

She was not particularly nervous. There were just a couple of butterflies floating around in her tummy, but Mummy and Daddy always said that it was good to have a couple—it meant that you cared. She had explained all about the test to her parents when she spoke to them on Sunday evening.

"That's ghastly, darling," her mother declared. "We'll come and get you straight away. You were accepted into the school and they can't ask you to do a test now. It's simply not fair."

"It's all right, Mummy. I've studied with Miss Reedy and I can only do my best," she replied.

Her father was far more sensible. "Sweetheart, if you'd like to come home, you know we'll support you. But remember, you are a Highton-Smith-Kennington-Jones. Not a family of quitters. I'm sure that you'll blitz the test. Just do your best. Besides, I imagine the headmistress has a very good reason for asking you to do it."

Alice-Miranda knew she could rely on her father to be reasonable. When her mother hopped back on the phone she had calmed down.

"All right, darling heart, we'll be thinking of you. You know that we'll be proud of you, whatever happens."

Alice-Miranda arrived at Miss Higgins's office with her pencil case. Miss Grimm had thought carefully about where she should sit for the test. Higgins seemed rather taken with the child and she had also spied Reedy talking to her in the quadrangle, looking far too happy. Neither of them could be trusted to supervise. She had come to the very unsettling conclusion that there was no one who could be trusted not to help the little brat. In the end Ophelia had decided that the child must sit the test at the writing table in Ophelia's own study. It was the only way she could be sure that Alice-Miranda didn't cheat. The thought of having her in the room created a tingling discomfort that started in the soles of her feet and finished at the ends of her hair. But it had to be done.

"Hello, Miss Higgins." Alice-Miranda let herself into the office.

"Oh, hello, Alice-Miranda." For once Miss Higgins did not seem ready to fall off her chair. "I've been expecting you. Are you ready to do the test?"

"As ready as I can be." Alice-Miranda smiled and looked around the room. "Where would you like me to sit?"

"I thought you could sit over there at the writing table." Alice-Miranda headed for the table and began to pull out the chair. "But I have received a message that you're to do the test in . . . *there*." Miss Higgins mouthed the word *there* silently and pointed at the double doors which led into Miss Grimm's study.

"Really?" Alice-Miranda hastily pushed the chair back under the writing table. "That's lovely." She smiled. "I will be so glad to see Miss Grimm again. It's been over a week and I have really missed our chats."

"I don't think she's going to be in the mood for a

chat, Alice-Miranda. In fact, she asked me to explain that you are not to speak to her at all before or during the test," Miss Higgins said, and shook her head. "She was very specific."

"Did she say anything about after the test?" Alice-Miranda was bouncing on the spot like Tigger.

"Well, no she didn't." Miss Higgins tapped her right forefinger to her lips and tried to mask a smile.

"There you are. I promise I'll not say a word—well, not unless she asks me something—before and during the test. But I will talk to Miss Grimm afterward." Alice-Miranda beamed.

"I really think you shouldn't. She's been quite upset." Miss Higgins led the way to the door. "Come on, then, let's get you in there and get it over with."

Miss Higgins knocked three times and turned the brass handle.

"Come," Miss Grimm's voice boomed from deep inside.

Miss Higgins motioned for Alice-Miranda to enter. But first she grabbed her wrists. "Good luck, sweetheart," she whispered.

"Thank you." Alice-Miranda skipped through the doorway.

Chapter 28

"There." Miss Grimm pointed at the writing table adjacent to the bookcase. It was far enough away from her own desk that she wouldn't be distracted, but the little brat would still be in full view.

Alice-Miranda skipped to the chair and pulled it out. She sat up and began arranging her pencils.

"I hope you don't mind, Miss Grimm—"

"SILENCE! Didn't that stupid woman tell you that you are not to speak to me before or during the test?" Miss Grimm roared, her voice shaking.

"Ye–" Alice-Miranda suppressed the urge to answer and simply nodded.

"Then don't speak," Miss Grimm commanded, arching her left eyebrow.

Alice-Miranda sat at her desk and tried to remember some of the things she had studied with Miss Reedy. She glanced down at the carpet and saw two very stylish black shoes, rather like a pair her mother had at home. She was about to say something but stopped herself just in time.

"This test has been designed, by me, to see if you are worthy of a place here at Winchesterfield-Downsfordvale," Miss Grimm began. She stood ramrod straight beside the desk but not close enough that Alice-Miranda could have reached out and touched her.

"You have three hours. You may not ask me any questions, at all, about anything. Do you understand?"

Alice-Miranda nodded again. Miss Grimm set the paper down in front of her.

It looked like a book rather than a test paper. She glanced up at Miss Grimm, not wanting to start before she was supposed to.

"Well, are you going to start or are you going to sit there staring at it?" Miss Grimm barked.

Alice-Miranda wrote her name on the front page. She smiled then, as she realized that Miss Grimm would automatically know who it belonged to, seeing as she was the only one taking the test.

"Something amusing?" Miss Grimm glared at Alice-Miranda from the safety of her desk, to which she had immediately retreated.

Alice-Miranda shook her head, her eyes fixed firmly on the paper in front of her.

"Then I suggest you get on with it. You may find it a little . . . challenging," Miss Grimm sneered.

Alice-Miranda opened the booklet and flicked through the whole document before she began. It was divided into subjects. English included sections on spelling, reading comprehension, grammar and writing. That was followed by mathematics. She spied a couple of rather difficult-looking long divisions. Next came geography, then science, art and last of all history. It was a very long paper indeed. Alice-Miranda knew that she would have to make sure she left enough time for each section so she quickly added up that three hours equal 180 minutes, which divided by six sections gave her thirty minutes for each.

She took a deep breath and began. The first section on English was not too bad at all, although there were a couple of challenging vocabulary questions she had to think carefully about.

Write a sentence to indicate your understanding of the word deplorable.

Fortunately her granny used that word quite often when she was describing the standard of children's manners.

My granny thinks the manners of children today are utterly deplorable.

Alice-Miranda found that she completed the first section in less than the thirty minutes she had allowed—which was just as well, because some of the long divisions were tricky and took more time than she had hoped. The geography section proved a breeze. Alice-Miranda spent a lot of time traveling with her parents. A special hobby of her father's was to plot their route on a map and quiz Alice-Miranda about the names of the countries and various cities. Her heart practically leapt for joy when she saw the question about Rajasthan. Their dear friend Prince Shivaji lived just outside of the capital, Jaipur, in the most magnificent old palace.

Alice-Miranda was quite enjoying Miss Grimm's test. She glanced up at the clock to check how much time she had left. Three sections to go and ninety-two minutes.

The science section didn't trouble her much either.

At home when Mrs. Oliver wasn't busy cooking meals for the family or teaching Alice-Miranda how to cook, she liked to indulge her passion for home chemistry. Dolly often took Alice-Miranda down to the basement, where she had a laboratory set up. She was trying to invent a freeze-dried pasta sauce and various other nutritious supplements for adventurers. You see, many years before, her own husband had tragically died in his attempt to become the first man to walk the entire perimeter of Europe unassisted. Dolly always blamed herself for not packing him enough nourishing foods. Alice-Miranda had only to think of all the experiments she and Mrs. Oliver had conducted, and the science section was done.

Art was one of Alice-Miranda's favorite subjects. From a very young age she had loved nothing more than spending an afternoon with her mother wandering through galleries. Her favorite was the Louvre in Paris, although she liked it as much for the beautiful building as for the artwork inside.

The final section, history, took the least time to complete. There were questions about Ancient Rome, Ancient Egypt, the Second World War and finally about King Henry the Eighth. Alice-Miranda checked for spelling mistakes and read through the whole paper. She was satisfied that she had done her best, and that was all anyone could ask of her.

There were fifteen minutes left until her three hours were up. But Alice-Miranda felt that she had checked as much as she could. She turned to face Miss Grimm, who was sitting at her desk writing.

"I've finished, Miss Grimm," Alice-Miranda announced.

"Really?" Miss Grimm glanced at the clock on the wall. She supposed that the child had tired of it all and decided to give up. "Bring it to me," she commanded.

Alice-Miranda stood up and walked toward Miss Grimm. She was about to hand it to her when Miss Grimm pointed at the corner of the desk. "Leave it there," she barked.

"It was a lovely test, thank you, Miss Grimm. I really enjoyed it. There were so many interesting words and the questions were great fun." Alice-Miranda smiled.

Miss Grimm stared over the edge of her spectacles. "Fun? You thought the test was fun?"

"Oh yes, Miss Grimm. I loved that question about King Henry the Eighth and his wives. Wasn't he the most awful man? Fancy chopping off your wife's head when she upset you—how dreadful."

Miss Grimm had a most uncomfortable feeling in the pit of her stomach.

"Miss Grimm, ever since I came to Winchesterfield-Downsfordvale I have loved every minute. But I have this niggling worry and, well . . . it's all to do with you, really," explained Alice-Miranda.

Miss Grimm glared at this infernal child with her chocolate brown curls and eyes as big as saucers.

"Miss Grimm, may I ask why you never come out of your study? All the girls would love to see you. They miss you. I know you are terribly busy. It must be very demanding to run a school like this and do it so well."

Miss Grimm put her hand up to silence Alice-Miranda—but she would not be quiet.

"It's just that everyone needs you. I know Miss Higgins does a wonderful job delivering all your messages and things but it's you the girls want to see. And Mr. Charles and Howie and Mrs. Smith—when she gets back from America, of course—and all the teachers must want to see you too."

Alice-Miranda walked around to Miss Grimm's side of the desk. She hesitated, then reached up and gently touched her shoulder. Miss Grimm recoiled as though she had just been hit with forty thousand volts. She leapt from her chair and ran toward the door at the other end of the study. Alice-Miranda could have sworn she heard a sob as Miss Grimm threw open the door.

"Get out of my study!" she screamed, turning around. "Get out and do not come back!" Miss Grimm disappeared through the door, slamming it behind her.

"I'm sorry, Miss Grimm, I didn't mean to upset you," Alice-Miranda whispered.

Chapter 29

Alice-Miranda let herself out of the study.

Miss Higgins looked up from her typing and saw Alice-Miranda's forlorn face. "Oh, dear girl, was it really that bad?"

"No, not at all. The test was great fun and I told Miss Grimm that myself," she replied.

"Well, what is it, then?" Miss Higgins stood up and walked toward Alice-Miranda. She took her hand and led her to the settee in the corner.

"I've upset Miss Grimm. I didn't mean to. It's just that, well, I asked her why she doesn't come out of her study. I told her that we all miss her and that the girls and the teachers and all the other staff would love to see her and then . . ." Alice-Miranda hesitated.

"And then?" Miss Higgins prompted.

"She ran out of the study through that doorway at the end and I think she was crying. I mean, she yelled at me, which is quite usual, but I could have sworn that she was upset." Alice-Miranda stared into Miss Higgins's eyes.

"Don't blame yourself, Alice-Miranda. She'll be fine. I'm sure she'll be back to her old self in no time at all," Miss Higgins said reassuringly. However, privately she wondered if perhaps something *had* changed.

"Whatever happened to Miss Grimm, Miss Higgins? Why does she hide away from everyone? Winchesterfield-Downsfordvale is such a wonderful school but she doesn't get to enjoy any of it at all. I don't understand." Alice-Miranda sat back against the frame of the couch.

"I'm sorry, sweetheart, but it's not something I can discuss," Miss Higgins replied. She wanted to tell Alice-Miranda about Miss Grimm. She wanted to tell her *everything*. But Alice-Miranda was just a child and she didn't need that burden. She wanted to tell her that Miss Ophelia Grimm had once been the most stylish and outgoing woman in the school. She had roamed around the grounds talking to the staff, admiring their work, chatting with the girls and teachers. She had had girls into her study for tea and laughed as they recounted their mishaps in the science room and at camp. She had been so young and so happy. And then she had fallen in love.

"Will you tell her that I'm sorry I upset her?" Alice-Miranda asked quietly.

"Of course, dear girl. Now, you must be starving. I know that Mrs. Oliver has baked a special cake for you. In honor of finishing that test. Why don't you run along to the dining room? I'll be down shortly."

Miss Higgins stood up, took Alice-Miranda's hand and directed her to the doorway. She opened the door and watched her go. Alice-Miranda looked back and smiled.

"Thank you, Miss Higgins." She turned and headed off down the hallway.

Chapter 30

Alice-Miranda walked quickly to the dining room. It was after eleven a.m. and she was late for morning tea. Her tummy gurgled noisily and she was looking forward to whatever treat Mrs. Oliver had whipped up.

The dining room rattled and chinked with the usual sounds of teacups and cutlery. But as she entered, Millie—who had been keeping one eye on the doorway—jumped up and shouted, "She's back!"

Immediately Jacinta Headlington-Bear leapt onto her chair and shouted, "Three cheers for Alice-Miranda. Hip, hip, hooray! Hip, hip, hooray! Hip, hip, hooray!"

Alice-Miranda could hardly believe the scene in front of her. She was suddenly bombarded with questions.

"What was it like?"

"Was it hard?"

"How do you think it went?"

She hardly had time to catch her breath.

"When are you getting kicked out?" Alethea snarled.

"Yes, when are you getting kicked out?" the three marionettes echoed. Alethea shot them a stare and they immediately sat down.

The room finally settled and Alice-Miranda began to speak. She was so little that the girls couldn't see her. Much to everyone's surprise, Mr. Plumpton grabbed a chair and lifted Alice-Miranda onto it.

"Thank you, Mr. Plumpton," Alice-Miranda said. His nose glowed red and he smiled awkwardly. "Thanks, everyone. The test was great. I rather enjoyed it and I hope that I have done quite well. But I suppose I will just have to wait and see."

Miss Reedy smiled at Alice-Miranda from the teachers' table.

"Well, young lady, now it's time for morning tea." Mr. Plumpton picked her up and set her back down on the floor.

"Goodness, I hope you haven't been waiting for me," Alice-Miranda gasped.

"Yes, we have," said Alethea. "Reedy said that we should wait until you got back because you've had to do a big test—poor little pet."

"Well, that was very kind of her and of you all." Alice-Miranda smiled at Alethea, who rolled her eyes and looked away.

Morning tea was delicious. Mrs. Oliver hadn't cooked just one cake. She'd cooked four different types and they were all favorites of Alice-Miranda's. There was devil's food cake, which is the most delicious chocolate concoction, hazelnut torte, sponge cake filled with cream, and strawberry butterfly cupcakes.

Afterward the girls were given an extra half-hour of playtime before they had to return to class. Miss Reedy asked Alice-Miranda to come to her study. Alice-Miranda went through the test—well, as much as she could remember.

"My dear girl, it sounds as though you have done very well." Miss Reedy sat staring at this simply amazing child. "Let's hope that Miss Grimm gives you the results soon and doesn't make you wait too long."

"Yes, I hope so," Alice-Miranda agreed.

"Now, as I understand, the next part of your program involves a rather strenuous physical challenge.

I've asked Charlie if he can give you some lessons on setting up your tent and getting a fire started—those outdoorsy type things which I assume you haven't had a lot of experience with," said Miss Reedy, glancing at her watch.

"Well, to tell you the truth, Miss Reedy, I have been camping a few times. You see, Daddy helps out with an organization that builds schools for children in different parts of Africa. The last two times he has been he took me and it was wonderful. He taught me how to put up the tent and to build a fire and to cook my own meals. It's funny, but Daddy said that everyone should know how to look after themselves. But I don't suppose he thought I would need those skills just yet," she finished with a grin.

"That's wonderful, but I'm sure it wouldn't hurt for you to have a refresher with Charlie this afternoon," said Miss Reedy.

"What about my lessons?" Alice-Miranda asked.

"The faculty have decided that there is really not much point in your having your lessons until we know that you are staying for good. Better to spend the time preparing for your Wilderness Walk and then your sporting match." Miss Reedy picked up the telephone on her desk and dialed the number for the greenhouse.

"Hello, Charlie, it's Livinia Reedy. I have Alice-Miranda with me now. Should I send her to you?" she asked in a rather clipped and businesslike manner. "Yes, now would be perfect. She will be there in five minutes."

Alice-Miranda stood up. "I suppose I should be going," she said.

"Yes, and work hard, my dear. Although it sounds like you have had lots of camping experience for a child your age, I'm sure that Charlie can teach you a few new tricks."

Alice-Miranda thanked Miss Reedy and let herself out the door.

Meanwhile, Miss Grimm sat in the depths of her wardrobe with a mountain of tissues at her side. She had broken her cardinal rule. She had been un-masked. Through a haze of tears she had tracked Alice-Miranda as she left the office and headed to the dining room. The ridiculous scene that followed was more than a little disconcerting. Then Livinia had taken the girl back to her study. Unfortunately that room did not have cameras. It was not a place where Ophelia had expected to need intervention—but she was wrong. The little brat had got to Reedy. Of all people, reliable Reedy; an English teacher of great renown who wore no emotion on any sleeve.

But it seemed that they were all against her. Winchesterfield-Downsfordvale had routines. There were things that happened and things that didn't. Staff knew their places and they just got on with it. It didn't matter whether they were happy or not. As long as the results were achieved then no one would question a thing. They would leave her alone and she could run the school as she saw fit. But this child, this tiny girl with chocolate curls and eyes as big as saucers, had set everything on its head. She had even seen that mad musician Mr. Trout laughing in the quadrangle with a group of girls. Outrageous behavior indeed.

Ophelia left the wardrobe and went to wash her face. She would need to look at the examination paper at some stage. She straightened her blazer, smoothed her skirt and strode back into the study, determined not to let Alice-Miranda upset her any further. The paper lay on her desk, exactly where the child had set it down.

Ophelia sat in her leather chair and reached for the paper. *Alice-Miranda Highton-Smith-Kennington-Jones* was printed neatly across the top of the front page. As if I wouldn't know it belonged to her, Ophelia thought. Twit. She turned the page and began to read. Red pen in hand, she prepared to unleash inky fireworks all over the page. But a surge of disappointment rose from the bottoms of her feet. The first answer was correct, and the second and the third. In fact, there was nothing on the first page to warrant any response other than a tick. Ophelia's immediate thought was that the girl must have cheated. But she had sat not three meters from Ophelia's own desk, and she herself had watched the girl most of the time. She must have had some sort of radio microphone with Reedy feeding her the answers.

But in her heart Ophelia Grimm knew that wasn't true. Livinia Reedy would never risk her reputation in that way—not even for this child.

She read on. The answers weren't just correct, they were detailed and they were insightful and . . . they were incredible. At the end of the paper she folded her arms on her desk, and then raised one hand on which to rest her head. Ninety-seven percent. She hesitated before writing the mark on the top right-hand corner of the front cover. Apart from one long division question, the entire paper was correct. She slid the test into her bottom drawer. She would give the results after the next two tasks. It was best not to give the brat false hope.

Chapter 31

Alice-Miranda spent the afternoon with Charlie. She unrolled and pitched a tent; then he showed her how to take it down and refold it to fit neatly back into the bag. He was amazed when she gathered kindling for a fire, set the fireplace with rocks and even managed to get some sparks to start it.

He showed her pictures of plants she could eat if she lost her own food supplies and, more importantly, he showed her all the things that she shouldn't touch lest they make her sick or give her hives. Alice-Miranda asked loads of questions and made sure that she understood everything he told her. Going camping with her father was one thing, but being alone in the forest for five days was another entirely.

As Alice-Miranda knelt beside the fireplace, carefully smothering the last sparks with a handful of sand, Charlie knelt down opposite her. He knew she was more than capable of completing Miss Grimm's challenge, but there was something troubling him. It had started with the broken orchid and the crumpled blanket in the greenhouse. He hadn't made much of it at the time; probably some of the girls sneaking about after dark, he'd thought. Even the next day when he found cake crumbs and an empty bottle of ginger beer in the rowing shed it hadn't worried him greatly. But then last night there was a shadow outside the greenhouse. Too big to be one of the girls and too late to be any of the staff. It was a man for sure, a hobo perhaps. Probably not dangerous, just hungry and tired, he had told himself.

Alice-Miranda's big brown eyes met Charlie's blue gaze. "Is there something the matter, Mr. Charles?" she asked, puzzled. "You look awfully serious. Did I do something wrong?"

"No, no, child. You've done everything just right," he sighed.

"I'm excited, you know. And just a little bit nervous,"

she admitted. "It's quite a challenge Miss Grimm has set for me. But I know I can do it."

Charlie thought for a moment. He didn't want to frighten her, but he did want her to be extra careful.

"Well, lass, you take good care of yourself out there and if there's any trouble, you just come straight back to school."

Alice-Miranda reached across and squeezed Charlie's hand.

"Oh, Mr. Charles, don't you worry about me. I will be just fine. There's nothing out there to hurt me. Goodness, there are no lions or elephants at Winchesterfield-Downsfordvale, I'm sure."

Charlie stood up and dusted himself off. For some reason he felt better. If there was a hobo, he'd likely have his hands full if he came across Miss Alice-Miranda.

"Now," he said, "Mrs. Oliver said that she has some special food she wants you to try out."

Alice-Miranda brushed the sand from her hands. "Oh, I know what that will be! Did you know that under our house she has her own laboratory? She experiments with all sorts of foods. I think she must have made some progress on her freeze-dried lamb roast with spring vegetables." Alice-Miranda licked her lips at the thought of Dolly's roast.

"She said she could give you enough food for a month and that it wouldn't weigh any more than what you would usually take for a couple of days. The woman must be a genius," said Charlie, in a very admiring tone.

Alice-Miranda said goodbye to Charlie and headed for the kitchen. Dolly had a range of foods for her to sample—except they didn't look like food at all to begin with.

"Hello, Mrs. Oliver." Alice-Miranda bounded into the kitchen, straight into Dolly's arms.

"Hello, my darling girl," Mrs. Oliver said, hugging her gently. "Did you enjoy your tea this morning?"

"Delish. I loved the devil's food cake—one of your best ever, I'd say."

"Yes, pity about the cream buns," Dolly muttered under her breath.

"Cream buns?" Alice-Miranda replied.

"Never mind, dear. There are some days I think I might be losing my marbles." Mrs. Oliver shook her head.

Alice-Miranda smiled. "That's silly," she said. "You're the sanest person I've ever met. Now, what is it that you want me to taste?"

Dolly moved to the long stainless-steel bench,

where she had several small mounds of what looked to be dried beans laid out on a series of plates.

"You know I've been working on freeze-dried recipes, so that people who go off on camps, or adventurers like my dear Dougal, God rest his soul, will have enough nutritious food to survive for extended periods?" She moved toward the stove, where several shallow pans of water hissed and boiled.

"Yes, I thought you were making some great progress last time I was in the lab," Alice-Miranda enthused.

"Well, my dear girl, I've done it. I have managed to take a whole roast dinner and freeze-dry it into these few beans." Dolly scooped up one of the piles and held them in her hand for Alice-Miranda to see.

"That, there, will turn into a roast?" Alice-Miranda looked at her in disbelief.

"Just watch this." Dolly dropped the beans into one of the boiling pans. Within a minute the water had evaporated and there in the pan for all to see was a roast lamb dinner, complete with baked potatoes, pumpkin, peas, carrots and brussels sprouts.

"That's incredible!" Alice-Miranda gasped.

"Go on." Dolly pushed her forward and handed her a fork. "Taste it."

Alice-Miranda took the fork from Dolly and gently pierced one of the small potatoes. She held up the steaming vegetable and blew on it before biting through the crisp outer skin.

Alice-Miranda chewed and swallowed. "That's fantastic. I can't believe it. You'll be famous the world over."

"I don't care about the fame, my love. It's about looking after people and making sure that they have enough food to eat. Your father told me it has all sorts of possibilities for people in needy places, as long as they don't mind a roast." Dolly wiped a small splodge of gravy from the corner of Alice-Miranda's lip.

"I'm sure that you could freeze-dry other dinners too, things people from other countries would prefer to eat," Alice-Miranda said, before she cut a small piece of lamb and pushed it onto her fork with a bright orange carrot.

"I'll show you the next one." Mrs. Oliver dropped another pile of beans into a pan. "This one's roast pork."

It seemed that there was quite a range in Dolly's collection. She had roast lamb, roast pork and roast beef, but the most amazing of all was yet to come. She had also developed a range of puddings to go with the dinners. When she produced a chocolate pudding, followed by a ginger pudding, followed by a plum pudding (for adventurers who might be out at

Christmastime), Alice-Miranda was truly astounded. Not only did they look great, they tasted even better. Alice-Miranda had a spoonful of each and decided she had better not have any more or she would spoil her dinner.

"So there you have it, my dear girl. You can have a roast dinner every night that you have to be out on that wretched hike." Mrs. Oliver began clearing away the pots.

"Thank you, that's marvelous. Although I should like to try cooking some rice for myself as well," said Alice-Miranda, looking up at the huge canisters of ingredients.

"I can pack some for you. I just want to make sure you don't have too much to carry. You are only small, sweetheart, and you already have to take the tent and a sleeping bag and clothes. At least the freeze-dried dinners don't weigh much." By now Mrs. Oliver was up to her elbows scrubbing pots in the sink.

Alice-Miranda grabbed a tea towel and began drying a saucepan.

"Get off with you, girl." Mrs. Oliver wiped her brow with the back of her pink-gloved hand. "I've plenty of help in here. You go and spend some time with Millie and your friends. You've worked far too hard today already."

Alice-Miranda did as she was told. She finished wiping the saucepan and sat it on the bench. Just as she was about to head out, Charlie appeared at the door.

"Oh, hello, Mr. Charles, you should see what Mrs. Oliver has invented. It's incredible. I'll be able to eat like a princess while I'm on my hike," she chattered as he kicked off his boots before entering the kitchen.

"That's wonderful, lass. I just thought I'd pay a visit and see if there might be any more of that chocolate cake from this morning."

Alice-Miranda could have sworn she saw Mr. Charles wink at Mrs. Oliver. Mrs. Oliver was suddenly bright red—and not just from the steaming kitchen sink, it would seem.

Chapter 32

The next few days passed quickly. Alice-Miranda spent more time with Charlie learning camp craft and preparing for her hike. Fortunately she would be able to stay on the school grounds the whole time, as it occupied an enormous piece of land with varied terrain. There was a forest and some mountains, open countryside and a stream.

On Thursday, Miss Reedy met Alice-Miranda just after breakfast and introduced her to the school sports teacher, Miss Benitha Wall. Miss Wall was impossibly tall and equally square. Alice-Miranda had to lay her head back as far as she could to see Miss Wall's face. Apparently she had competed most successfully in wrestling, shot put and discus at the Olympics. That wasn't a surprise in the least.

"Alice-Miranda, Miss Wall will help you prepare for your sporting match. Have you given any thought to what you would like to compete in?" Miss Reedy asked.

"Well, Miss Reedy, I know a few sports that I won't be trying. Gymnastics, for example—no one could beat Jacinta. And it won't be running because I'm not very fast and I can't run for a long time either, so cross country is off the list. I'm all right at tennis but I don't think my forehand would stand up to Millie's ground strokes."

"Are you a swimmer?" Miss Wall bent down so that she could meet Alice-Miranda's eyes.

"I'm afraid not. I like swimming but I haven't trained enough to be competitive. And no offense, Miss Wall, but I don't think I have quite the right frame to be attempting any field sports." Alice-Miranda sighed. This was harder than she had expected.

"Do you ride?" Miss Reedy inquired.

"Oh yes, I have a lovely pony called Bonaparte. Daddy calls him Bony Pony but I can tell you he eats so much there is no possibility of spying any bones on that boy. I decided that when I came to school he could have a good spell, so he's at home being thoroughly spoiled. It wouldn't be fair to bring him in—I told him he could have at least three months off playing."

Alice-Miranda thought for a few moments longer and then her eyes lit up. "I know! I love sailing and Daddy bought me a little skiff. I called her *Emerald* because she is the most beautiful green. Could we have a sailing regatta on the lake?"

"That's a wonderful idea," Miss Reedy agreed. "We must phone your parents and see if they can have your sailboat sent up at once. You need to have some days to practice."

"But do any of the other girls sail?" Alice-Miranda asked.

"We had a regatta on the lake last year. The winner was named the school champion and given a trophy. Funny thing was, all the girls were fairly terrible at sailing and this girl only won because everyone else ended up in the reeds or sank," Miss Wall laughed.

"That means I should at least have a chance," Alice-Miranda smiled. "I mean, I'm not brilliant but I have had a few lessons."

Miss Reedy seemed lost in her thoughts. She said that she would have to consult the school records to see who won the regatta. Suddenly she seemed to remember.

"Are you sure about this, Alice-Miranda?" Miss Reedy asked ominously.

"Yes, Miss Reedy. Really, I can't think of anything else. Why? Do you remember who the school champion is?" Alice-Miranda was wide-eyed.

"Yes I do. And I'm afraid that it's someone who would do anything to beat you," her teacher replied.

"Alethea?" Alice-Miranda asked.

Miss Reedy nodded slowly.

Miss Wall nodded too. "I remember now. She had her father buy her a brand-new boat and he had it shipped here just before the race. It was a real beauty, but by the end of the weekend she had made a right mess of it. She said that she didn't want to sail ever again."

"That could work in your favor, Alice-Miranda. The fact that she's not actually a skilled sailor and she doesn't particularly like sailing may give you a small advantage," said Miss Reedy. "Although we all know that Miss Goldsworthy will go to extraordinary lengths to win," she finished in a whisper.

"Well, I'll just have to beat her fair and square. I'll call Daddy now and see if he can send my boat straight away. Then I might have a few days to get out on the lake before I have to go on camp."

Alice-Miranda marched off to phone her parents.

{187}

Miss Reedy and Miss Wall shook their heads and smiled.

"There's never been one like her before," Miss Wall laughed.

"Yes, and that's why we absolutely can't let her fail."

Chapter 33

“**I** can’t believe that Grimm *still* hasn’t told you your test results,” said Millie, as she lay on her bed with her legs pointed at right angles to the ceiling.

“Well, I suppose Miss Grimm has her reasons. I was going to head over and see her about it, but then I thought that perhaps she wants to tell me after I have been on the camp and competed in the regatta.” Alice-Miranda hugged Brummel Bear to her chest.

It was late on Sunday afternoon. Alice-Miranda was packed, ready to head off on her hike the next day. She’d had lots of lessons in map reading and using the compass. But she wouldn’t receive the final route until later that evening, when Miss Higgins was to deliver her map from Miss Grimm.

"Mrs. Smith should be back soon," said Alice-Miranda.

"Who?" Millie asked.

"Mrs. Smith. You know, Cook." Alice-Miranda rolled onto her stomach to face Millie.

"Oh no. I hope this trip has put her in a better mood . . . and that she's had some cooking lessons while she's been away. Her food is gross." Millie screwed up her face and poked a finger down her throat.

"Mrs. Oliver has agreed to stay on for another week or so, until Mrs. Smith settles back in. I'm sure she'll appreciate the company and someone else to help with the meals." Alice-Miranda glanced out the window and noticed a beam of light, which seemed to be heading toward the field.

"There's Birdy now!" She jumped up and ran to the window. "Come on, Millie, let's go and see how she is. I want to say hello to Cyril too." Alice-Miranda slipped her feet into her shoes and threw a jumper over her head. The familiar *chop-chop-chop* of Birdy's whirring blades filled the twilight air. By the time the helicopter had landed on the lower oval Alice-Miranda and Millie were ready to pounce. The helicopter's engine shuddered to a halt. Cyril placed his headset on the dashboard, hopped out and retrieved a suitcase from the rear.

At first Alice-Miranda didn't recognize the tall woman with the fashionable brown hair who emerged from the chopper.

"Who's that?" Millie frowned. "It's not Cook."

As she approached, Alice-Miranda realized that it was indeed Mrs. Smith. Her bent frame was upright and she had a very nice new hairdo. Even her skin seemed to be glowing. Alice-Miranda ran forward to greet her.

"Hello, Mrs. Smith." She wrapped her arms around the stylish woman.

"Oh, my dear girl, hello to you too," Mrs. Smith replied. A wide smile beamed from her face and Millie realized for the first time that Mrs. Smith was actually quite attractive for an older woman.

"Hello, Millicent," Mrs. Smith said warmly.

"Welcome back, Cook." Millie smiled too.

The pilot was securing the helicopter. "Hello, Cyril," said Alice-Miranda.

"Hello, Alice-Miranda," he called back.

"When you've finished doing your checks on Birdy you must come up for a cup of tea. Mrs. Oliver is looking forward to seeing you."

"I'll be there shortly," he replied.

Alice-Miranda turned back to Mrs. Smith. "So, how was your trip? You must tell us all about it." She grabbed Mrs. Smith's hand and they began to walk toward the kitchen.

"I simply don't know where to begin!" she replied.

"Mrs. Oliver has baked something special as a welcome-home treat. How about a snack, and *then* you can tell us everything?"

They reached the door and Alice-Miranda called, "Hello, Mrs. Oliver, Mrs. Smith's back." She opened the screen and let herself and the others inside. The most delicious smell hovered in front of the oven. Mrs. Oliver emerged from the pantry. Although she and Mrs. Smith had met each other briefly, this was their first proper meeting and Mrs. Oliver was a little nervous. Mrs. Smith had a formidable reputation among the staff and girls and it was not for her cooking.

"Good evening, Mrs. Smith." Mrs. Oliver held out her hand.

Mrs. Smith took it and then steamed forward, enveloping Mrs. Oliver heartily. "You have made me the happiest woman in the world, Mrs. Oliver." A tear sprouted from her eye. "And you, Miss Highton-Smith-Kennington-Jones, to whom I may just be related somewhere a long time ago"—she scooped

Alice-Miranda into her arms—"you, my dear girl, have made me the happiest grandmother on earth."

Over tea and pound cake Mrs. Smith told her eager audience all about her grandchildren in America. She had taken them to Disneyland and gone to Grandparents' Day at their school. They visited the Grand Canyon and went to see the Empire State Building too. But most of all and best of all, her grandchildren now knew her. The real her, not just the granny on the telephone who sends cards and presents for Christmas and birthdays.

"Now, you must tell me everything that's been happening here too," she said over her second piece of cake. "I suppose I should really ask if I still have a job."

"Of course you do, Mrs. Smith. I told Miss Grimm as soon as I could. She's eaten all her meals and there haven't been any complaints at all. She knows that you're coming back and Mrs. Oliver was only here for two weeks." Alice-Miranda looked down and shook some imaginary crumbs from her lap. "Except, Mrs. Oliver is going to stay another week—if that's all right with you, of course. Miss Higgins thought that it was about time you had someone else to bounce your ideas off and Mummy and Daddy don't need Mrs. Oliver just yet." Alice-Miranda smiled hesitantly.

"I would be honored to have you by my side, Mrs. Oliver," Mrs. Smith announced.

"Well, in that case, Mrs. Smith, you must call me Dolly," Mrs. Oliver replied.

"And you must call me Doreen."

So it was settled. The two ladies nattered on like schoolgirls. Cyril soon appeared for a cup of tea and gave Alice-Miranda a full update on what was going on back home.

"Your parents are well but that pony of yours has been in a bit of strife," Cyril told them. It seemed that Bonaparte had escaped from his stable and somehow managed to get into the vegetable garden. He demolished half the cabbages before Mr. Greening caught up with him.

"Well, you know how that boy only has to look at rich food and he gets the colic, so Mr. Greening called the vet just in case," Cyril continued.

"Oh dear," Alice-Miranda sighed. "He's a very naughty boy. Is he all right?"

"Yes, he's fine but young Max—he's the stablehand," Cyril explained to Mrs. Smith, "reported that Bonaparte had a very windy night."

Millie roared laughing at the thought of Bony the farting pony. Alice-Miranda asked Cyril to send her love to everyone and tell them that she was having the most wonderful time. She would see them all at midterm.

Mrs. Oliver and Mrs. Smith finished their chat and began bustling about the kitchen.

"May I suggest, girls, that if you and the rest of this school would like to be fed this evening, you'd best be off. We have a lot to get done and there's not much time before dinner," said Mrs. Smith with a dry smile.

Millie and Alice-Miranda headed out the door.

"Gosh, that was amazing. She's so different," Millie gasped.

"Everyone needs a holiday sometime. I suppose Mrs. Smith just proved that," Alice-Miranda replied.

Chapter 34

After dinner Miss Higgins delivered the map from Miss Grimm and Alice-Miranda spent an hour going over it with Charlie. He thought it was a reasonable route, although he was a little concerned by the mountain trek, where the trails weren't especially well marked. Alice-Miranda assured him she would be fine. If she got really lost she would just wait it out in the one spot until the end of the week. Her backpack contained enough of Mrs. Oliver's freeze-dried baked dinners and desserts to last at least a month.

Before bed she telephoned her parents, who were in particularly good form.

"Hello, darling," her mother cooed. "Are you having a dreadful time? We can be there to pick you up straight away."

"No, Mummy, as I have told you every day since I arrived, I'm having a marvelous time and I love it here. Please stop asking me if I'm having a dreadful time," Alice-Miranda replied.

"All right, darling, I promise to stop. You know Daddy and I are only teasing. We're so proud of you." Alice-Miranda could tell her mother was smiling.

"Now, Mummy, I won't be able to call you until Friday night as I am off on my Wilderness Walk. Remember, I told you that Miss Grimm wants me to complete a twenty-kilometer hike and camp out for the week? Mr. Charles has been so helpful, showing me how to pack my tent and roll my sleeping bag and all those other things I need to know. I'm so glad Daddy took me to Africa too. Five days out on the grounds is a wonderful adventure. So please don't worry about me. If I don't come back at the end of the week, I know they will send a search party."

"I do think Miss Grimm's being a bit tough on you, darling, but she is the headmistress and I suppose she has her reasons. Anyway, your father tells me you will be absolutely fine and you know I trust his judgment," her mother went on. In fact, Cecelia

Highton-Smith had been aghast at the thought of her daughter's having to complete such an enormous challenge. But after speaking to her sister Charlotte, who reminded her of their own camping adventures at a similar age, she allowed herself to get used to the idea. Besides, Mrs. Oliver had reported that Alice-Miranda's preparations with Mr. Charles had been very thorough.

"Daddy wants to say hello, so I'll go now. Have a wonderful week, darling, and I'll look forward to hearing all about it on Friday night. Love you."

"Thank you, Mummy. I love you too." Alice-Miranda waited for her father's voice.

"Hello, sweetheart, how are things at school?" he purred.

"Wonderful, Daddy. Mrs. Oliver has had a tremendous time, and thank you for letting us keep her another week. You should have seen Mrs. Smith when she returned this afternoon. She was like a new person—all refreshed and looking rather fabulous too. She and Mrs. Oliver had tea together. I think Mrs. Oliver was a little nervous, having taken over her kitchen in such a rush, but they got on famously and Mrs. Smith is ever so glad to have Mrs. Oliver stay on." Alice-Miranda's voice fizzed with excitement as she reported her news. "They even insisted on calling each other Dolly and Doreen—and you know Mrs. Oliver doesn't invite just *anyone* to call her Dolly."

"That's such good news. I'm glad it worked out so well for everyone." His voice took a more serious tone. "Now, how are you feeling about that hike tomorrow?"

"Really good, Daddy. Mr. Charles has been helping me prepare and I think I will be absolutely fine. Mrs. Oliver has packed me a load of her freeze-dried meals, so as long as I can get the fire going I'll be eating like a princess," Alice-Miranda replied.

But Alice-Miranda sounded more confident than she felt. She knew she was well prepared. But just in the past few days she had acquired an uneasy feeling. Not the same one she had when she first arrived; this was different—like there was someone about, watching. First there was the crumpled blanket in the potting shed and then Mrs. Oliver had complained a couple of times about cakes going missing from the kitchen. Alice-Miranda shook the idea from her head. She wasn't about to tell anyone—she had an adventure ahead.

"Well, you just take care," said her father. "It will be a splendid opportunity to write in your diary, and make sure that you take your camera too. We'll look forward to hearing all about your adventure on Friday night. And if you get into any real trouble you know you can always activate the emergency button on your phone and we'll be there straight away."

Alice-Miranda hesitated for a moment. "Actually, Daddy, I was planning to leave my phone here at school. I don't think I'll need it and I don't even want to be tempted if things get a little tricky or I get a bit lonely. I need to do this on my own—to prove to Miss Grimm that I really do belong here." She held her breath and waited for her father's reply.

He was silent for a moment. "Hmm. I've seen how good you are at camping and hiking, but it is still a big adventure to have on your own. If you're sure about it, I believe you can do it. But perhaps we just won't tell Mummy. You know she can be such a worrier."

His confidence buoyed Alice-Miranda's spirits. "Thank you, Daddy. I knew you'd understand—you of all people, who's climbed every major peak in the world and backpacked across South America. And back in those days mobile phones hadn't even been invented!" She couldn't help laughing.

"Thank you for reminding me how terribly old I am, sweetheart," her father replied, laughing too. "Now you'd better get some sleep. We will talk to you on

Friday evening when you are back safe and sound. Love you, darling."

"Love you too, Daddy." And with that Alice-Miranda rang off.

The next morning she awoke just a little earlier than usual. The plan was to have breakfast with the girls in the dining room and then head out. She hopped out of bed and went to have a shower and get dressed. On her way back to the dorm she bumped into Howie, who was about to start the wake-up rounds.

"Hello, Alice-Miranda, all ready for your big adventure?" asked the house mistress with a smile.

"Yes, I think I am," Alice-Miranda replied.

"It's going to be awfully quiet around this place without you," Howie said, and frowned.

"It will be over in a blink, Howie. I'm really rather excited." Alice-Miranda grinned broadly. But there *was* a little flutter in her tummy.

"Take care, my poppet. I will hear all about it on Friday evening." Howie leaned forward and hugged Alice-Miranda. Unbeknown to either of them, Alethea saw the whole thing from her bedroom doorway.

"Brat," she muttered under her breath.

Howie continued down the corridor and Alice-Miranda headed for her bedroom.

"Hello, little girl." Alethea appeared from her hiding place. She folded her arms and blocked Alice-Miranda's path. Then in a ridiculous baby voice, she said, "Going on a big adventure, sweetie pie? Hope you don't get lost out there."

"Oh, hello, Alethea." Alice-Miranda smiled back. "Yes, big adventure, but I am so looking forward to it. I've read the map, my backpack is packed and I think everything will be fine."

"What's wrong with you?" Alethea demanded. "Camping on your own in the forest for five days! I'd rather cut my toenails with an axe. Are you mad or just completely delirious?"

"But it's an adventure," Alice-Miranda said hesitantly.

"*An adventure,*" Alethea mimicked. "Well, good luck, little girl. Last year on the junior camp that idiot Jacinta saw a headless highwayman, a band of gypsies and an escaped convict. I wonder how many loonies will be out there after you," she whispered. "Probably just the one who's been stealing cakes and sleeping in the rowing shed. Or so I've heard." Alethea's eyes widened.

"I don't believe in ghosts and I've always found

gypsies to be the nicest people and, well, if I do come across any escaped criminals I'll be sure to take extra care," Alice-Miranda replied.

Alethea snorted. "By the way, I'm so glad that you decided to pick sailing for your sporting challenge. Daddy's sending up a new skiff for me tomorrow. It's a special one built for the Olympics and he says that the most ordinary sailor in the whole world would win in it."

Millie appeared behind Alethea, on her way to the bathroom.

"That's just as well, then, seeing as you're particularly ordinary at sailing," Millie interrupted. "Excuse me, Alethea, would you mind moving?"

Alethea turned around and glared. Her eyes were like winter frost on bare toes. "Why? Are you busting? I was just warning your little friend about all the bogeymen out there in the woods. Hope she doesn't get too scared and run back here to school."

"Oh, that's rich coming from you, Alethea!" The words were out of Millie's mouth before she had time to stop them.

"Why did you say that?" Alethea hissed.

"No reason. Now, will you let me through before I piddle on your doorstep?"

Alethea rolled her eyes and gave Millie a hefty shove before retreating into her bedroom.

"Why *did* you say that?" Alice-Miranda asked.

"The truth is Alethea's not exactly the school's best adventurer. Apparently the first year she was here she faked appendicitis when camp was on. Then the next year she told everyone her granny had died and she had to go home for the funeral, which was amazing because the very next week her granny was in the social pages. Then last year she couldn't come up with another excuse so she actually headed out and then phoned her father to send his helicopter to come and get her once the groups had split up. They dropped her back in on the last day and she emerged from the woods looking like she had spent all week out there. It's amazing what a bit of dirt and a few twigs can do," Millie sighed.

"But how do you know that?" Alice-Miranda was wide-eyed.

"Everyone heard the chopper, but nobody knew for sure until Ivory overheard Danika moaning to Shelby that it was so unfair she'd had to carry her own pack and Alethea's and Alethea had spent the whole week at the Downsfordvale Manor Spa having all sorts of posh body treatments, eating caviar and swanning about like Lady Muck," Millie replied.

"Did anyone tell the teachers?" asked Alice-Miranda.

"No, there was no point, really," Millie said with a sigh. "The Manor has a watertight confidentiality clause because of all the celebrities who go there, so there was no way to prove it."

Alice-Miranda shook her head. "Well, I promise that I won't be phoning Cyril. In fact, I've told Daddy that my phone is staying right here, safe in my drawer. No matter what happens I won't give up."

"That's the spirit. We know you can do it." Millie hugged her little friend and bounded off to the bathroom.

Chapter 35

A t breakfast Miss Reedy made the usual round of notices. At the end of the information about debating trials, music practices and sporting fixtures, she made one final announcement.

"May I take this opportunity to wish Alice-Miranda Highton-Smith-Kennington-Jones all the best for her Wilderness Walk adventure? Although we are not able to offer her bodily assistance, I'm sure that all of us will be there with her in spirit." Miss Reedy then asked Alice-Miranda to stand while Millie led the school in a rousing three cheers.

In the depths of her wardrobe Ophelia Grimm was watching the morning's antics. Although she couldn't hear what was going on in the dining room, she had a most uncomfortable feeling. She would have to tell those stupid men to hurry up and get the sound enabled in all areas—not just the assembly hall.

Her thoughts fixed on Alice-Miranda. Five days in the woods should sort her out. Ophelia had planned the route herself, setting what might only be described as a very challenging course indeed. The little brat had to retrieve a set of flags to prove she had covered the route exactly as it was marked. She had ordered Higgins to instruct Charlie to place the flags in the most difficult of places: the top of a tree, beside a beehive, in an animal hole. While he seemed somewhat soft in the head of late, with all that smiling and whistling, she still trusted him to do the right thing. Without his job at Winchesterfield-Downsfordvale, he had nothing.

The sight of almost the entire dining room clapping while that infernal pest stood up was more than a little disturbing. Although she did notice that Alethea, Danika, Shelby and Lizzy didn't seem the least taken in by her. Ophelia knew she'd made a fine choice in Alethea as Head Prefect. That girl could be relied on to do the right thing.

———

Alice-Miranda finished her breakfast and went outside to retrieve her pack. It seemed the whole school turned out to wave her goodbye.

Miss Higgins gave her a quick hug, as though she suspected someone might be watching, and shoved a small bar of chocolate into her hand. "A treat," she said, and smiled.

"Well then, lass, off with you." Mrs. Oliver hugged her too, then brushed a tear from her eye. Mrs. Smith did the same. She and Dolly smiled at each other with an unspoken understanding about this tiny girl with the chocolate curls.

Charlie walked with her across the lower oval to the gate.

"Bye," Millie called, waving furiously. A chorus of "Goodbye," "See you soon," "Good luck" and "You can do it" followed Alice-Miranda until the bell rang and the girls headed off to class.

Charlie dropped to one knee and met Alice-Miranda's eyes. "Now, lass, you know I have every faith in the world that you can survive out here for five days. But if you get into trouble, remember our plan and stay exactly where you are. If you are not back by four p.m. on Friday, I will be out there as fast as my legs can carry me."

"Thanks, Mr. Charles." Alice-Miranda reached out

and hugged him. "I'll see you on Friday," she called as she headed through the gate.

Charlie felt a stinging in his eyes. He brushed the moisture from his cheeks and smiled. Ever since that child had arrived he felt different. Better. Happy for the first time in a very long while.

Chapter 36

Alice-Miranda bounced along the track beside the stream. It didn't take too long before she found the first red flag, which was marked *Number 1*. She collected it from a low fork in an oak tree and placed it in the top of her pack. When she was tired, she rested; when she was hungry, she ate her snacks; and when the light was fading, she picked a camp-site, pitched her tent, built a fire and cooked herself some rice. By flashlight she wrote in her diary.

Monday
    A wonderful day. I'm rather tired now but I've
collected the first two of my flags and according

to the map I must have covered about 4 kilometers. For dinner I had some rice and soy sauce. It was delicious. I've cleaned my saucepan in the river and I think I will settle down to sleep quite soon. The trees are rustling gently and there are a few sounds I'm not sure about, but I know there's nothing out here that could hurt me.

Funny, but a few times I have felt rather like I was being watched. Maybe there really is someone out here—I know there have been stories. Or perhaps it's just because I am not used to being alone. School is so busy and at home there's always someone about.

Everyone at school has been so kind. But I am worried about Miss Grimm. As soon as I get back on Friday I will pop in and see her. I think she's lonely. Something terrible must have happened to make her so sad. If only she would come out and spend time with the girls and the teachers, then I know she would be happy again.

AMHSKJ

The next morning, Alice-Miranda washed her face in the river, packed up her belongings and ate her breakfast while consulting the map. Today she would begin the climb into the mountains, and the trails would become a little more difficult to follow.

Back at school, Miss Grimm wondered where Alice-Miranda might be. Crying in her tent was what she hoped, but she had a nagging feeling that perhaps that would not be the case.

Alice-Miranda walked all day, following her map and winding her way uphill. She collected another two flags and decided that she had traveled far enough. One of her flags was at the base of a tree that had a very large beehive hanging from a high branch. She wondered who had thought to put up the sign that said *Take care—beehive above*. She was extra cautious not to upset the bees and managed to get the flag without any bother at all.

All day she had had the nagging feeling that someone was watching her. She really did hope that it wasn't someone from school. Charlie knew how much she wanted to do this on her own, and she couldn't imagine that it was any of the teachers—and certainly none of the girls. As the afternoon sun began to sink over the inky mountains, Alice-Miranda selected a campsite and repeated her actions from the previous afternoon. While she was getting dinner from her pack she heard a rustling in the bushes. Her heart began to beat a little faster but she told herself not to be scared. She would be fine. As she emerged from her tent she thought she saw a figure move in the trees.

"Hello, is anyone there?" she called. "I'm going to cook some dinner and if you'd like to join me you're most welcome. But if that's you, Mr. Charles, please go home. I'm fine."

There was no reply, so Alice-Miranda set to, gathering some kindling from around the edge of the campsite. When she returned there was a little pile of rocks beside her tent.

"Thank you," she called. "If you'd like to join me I'll put two dinners on."

Alice-Miranda looked around and still couldn't see anyone. Strangely, she wasn't afraid. If this person had taken the time to collect some rocks for her to build a fire then she didn't think they would want to hurt her.

She retrieved her saucepan, filled it with water and put it on the fire to boil. When the water was simmering she tore open one of the packets and scattered the little beans into the pan. Within minutes the aroma of a fresh lamb roast filled the air.

Alice-Miranda thought that the smell might bring whoever was hiding out of their cover. But it didn't. She ate her dinner alone, the forest sounds her only company. Again she wrote in her diary before bed.

Tuesday

All day I had the same funny feeling that someone was watching me. I wasn't afraid—I felt more like they were willing me to go on. And now tonight I know that someone is around. They gathered some rocks and laid them beside the tent. When I asked them to join me for dinner, nobody came. Perhaps they will come out tomorrow.

I'm very tired. This afternoon I had a rather large thorn in my hand and although it was terribly sore, I managed to pull it out and apply some antiseptic and a bandage. The walking has been hard but the air is so clean and I feel very happy.

AMHSKJ

Alice-Miranda awoke with a start. The dawn light streamed through the gauze window above her head. She could have sworn there was a shadow but when she tore open the tent's zip she saw no one.

"Is anyone there? Please, you are most welcome to join me for breakfast. Don't be scared. I want to be your friend," she called. The poplars rustled gently in the breeze, the only answer to her questions.

Alice-Miranda ate her breakfast and packed up her

campsite. She studied the map and realized that today she would have to travel further than any other. The trail was densely wooded and the path was steep. As she walked, Alice-Miranda realized that she was climbing quite high.

Through a gap in the trees she glimpsed the whole of Winchesterfield-Downsfordvale laid out beneath her. It was breathtaking. She moved closer to the edge of the track to take some photographs and saw that the trail rose steeply from a rocky outcrop below. She edged forward carefully, leaving her pack behind her. A flat rock made the most wonderful seat and she sat taking in the view below and picking out all of the landmarks. There was the lake, the lower oval and the upper oval, the classrooms, the stables; she could even see where Miss Grimm's study was, below the tower in the main building. It was a glorious view.

With the sun on her face and a breath of wind behind her she closed her eyes and drank it all in. Suddenly a crunching sound made her jump, and her camera fell from her hands and wedged into some rocks below.

"Oh, blast!" she exclaimed. "Silly girl!" She reached out to try and get the camera but she was too small and it was too far away. The only solution was to climb down further. Alice-Miranda stood up and peered over the edge. It didn't look too far. Just as she was about to step off the platform a man's voice shouted.

"No! Amelia, no!"

Alice-Miranda steadied herself and only just managed to fall back onto the rock platform. A giant hand reached out and grabbed her arm and then she was back on the edge of the trail. She lay on the ground, squinting up at a man she had never seen before. The cut of his clothes was expensive but they were very dirty. His unshaven face, long hair and lean limbs gave him the appearance of a scrawny giant but there was something kind in his eyes. Alice-Miranda sat up. He stared at her intently, as though he was seeing the face of someone he had known a long time ago.

"Hello," she said quietly. "My name is Alice-Miranda Highton-Smith-Kennington-Jones and I am very pleased to meet you, Mr. . . . ?" She held out her hand.

The man stood still, just staring. It was as though he was unable to speak.

"Thank you for saving me. If you hadn't come along I could have tumbled all the way down there. It was very silly of me to take such a risk. Mr. Charles would have retrieved my camera for me when I went back to school." She tried again. "Do you have a name, sir?"

The man looked as though he was about to speak, gulped, but said nothing.

"I have some food, over there in my backpack." Alice-Miranda pointed to where she had left her pack in the bushes. "I could get you something." He looked as if he had not eaten properly for quite some time.

Alice-Miranda stood up, dusted herself off and slipped her hand into his. Without another word, she led him back along the trail to where she had left her things. There was a clearing with some rocks. She motioned that he should sit down. All the while he did not take his eyes off her.

Alice-Miranda decided that the man must be in shock, like when someone has an accident or they see something unexpected. A hint of brown material was poking out from behind a rock. She walked over to have a look and saw a tramp's stick, with his possessions tied into a bundled piece of fabric.

"Do you have a home, sir?" she asked.

He said nothing.

Alice-Miranda decided that the best thing she could do would be to give this poor fellow a strong cup of tea. But that required her to build a fire first. She quickly set about gathering rocks and kindling and soon had the last of her water boiling and hissing.

She handed him a tin mug and found a biscuit in her pack.

"Please, sir, a good strong cup of tea will have you feeling better in no time."

And so she sat down beside him and waited until he had a few sips. He turned to look at her. She smiled, her hair shining in the sunlight, her eyes dancing merrily.

"You're not Amelia," he said at last.

"No, sir, my name is Alice-Miranda Highton-Smith-Kennington-Jones. I go to Winchesterfield-Downsfordvale Academy for Proper Young Ladies and I am seven and one-quarter years old."

"But on the rock out there, for a moment you looked just like her," he whispered.

"Who do I look like?" she asked.

"It was a long time ago." He turned away, brushing a tear from his eye.

"Well, sir, I know that I'm only seven and one-quarter but I am a very good listener."

He turned to face her. There was something about her, not just that she looked like Amelia. He wanted to tell her things he hadn't told anyone before.

"My name is Aldous Grump and, a long time ago, I had a little girl called Amelia."

Alice-Miranda held out her tiny hand. "I am very pleased to meet you, Mr. Grump." She handed him a gingersnap biscuit.

Chapter 37

Aldous Grump told Alice-Miranda his story. He hadn't always been a tramp. Far from it, his life had been very busy. He had run a successful publishing company. He had married his wife, a beauty named Evelyn, when they were both young, and they had had a little girl, Amelia. She was everything he could have wanted in a daughter. She had cascading chocolate curls and eyes as big as saucers. And talk? She started when she was just nine months old and never seemed to stop. His life had been as near to perfect as any man's until his darling Evelyn was killed in a motor accident. Aldous thought he would never recover. He decided that the best thing for Amelia would be to send her to boarding school.

"I'm sure that was a very good idea," Alice-Miranda interrupted. "It would have been awfully hard to run your own business and look after Amelia too."

He nodded.

"Where did she go?" Alice-Miranda quizzed.

"Down there," said Aldous, looking toward the cliff top.

"Winchesterfield-Downsfordvale! My school!" Alice-Miranda exclaimed. "How wonderful. I'm sure that she had the most marvelous time. I have only been there for two weeks and I love it to bits. I came early, you know, and the whole reason I have to do this hike is to prove to Miss Grimm that I really should be there."

"Ophelia . . ." His voice broke and his shoulders slumped.

"Of course, you must know her too." Alice-Miranda smiled. "I think she's been there quite some time now."

"I didn't realize," he continued. "I thought she had gone."

"Oh no, she's very much in charge. She's a funny one, though. When I first arrived, Miss Higgins said that she hadn't been out of her study in over ten years. Well, I just thought that was ridiculous, so I have been to see her lots of times. She is on my mind quite a bit. When I first met her she seemed rather angry and not at all happy to see me. I didn't meet her before I came to the school, you see. Miss Higgins, her wonderful secretary, interviewed me and so it wasn't until I was already there that I thought I should pop in and introduce myself. I was worried about a few things. Mrs. Smith was sad because she had never been on holiday and Mr. Charles was upset about the flowers, and Jacinta Headlington-Bear, well, she was having the most ghastly tantrum. I suppose there was just a lot of unhappiness, and for not very good reasons. So I tried to help and most things are much better, but since then—and especially while I've been out here— I've been worrying dreadfully."

Mr. Grump looked up from the ground and into Alice-Miranda's eyes as she kept talking.

"Well, not about Mrs. Smith or Mr. Charles or Jacinta. You see, I've been worrying about Miss Grimm. I think she's actually terribly sad. She comes across all angry and upset and she's set all these tasks for me which none of the other girls have ever had to do, but I don't think she's really mean at all. I think she's miserable." Alice-Miranda finally took a breath.

Mr. Grump's eyes filled with tears. "It's my fault," he sobbed. "It's all my fault."

{221}

"That's silly. How could it be your fault? Your Amelia must have finished school a long time ago. I'm sure that she didn't make Miss Grimm sad."

Aldous took a deep breath. "When I met Ophelia she was lovely. She adored the girls and she took especially good care of my Amelia. We liked each other very much. Over time, we fell in love. I never thought I would love anyone after Evelyn, and here was this beautiful and clever young woman who loved me and loved my little daughter even more," he began.

"That's so romantic," Alice-Miranda sighed. She patted Mr. Grump gently on the shoulder.

"I asked her to marry me. She said yes and we began planning our wedding. Amelia was to be the flower girl in a beautiful pink dress. Ophelia was happier than I had ever seen her."

"What happened?" Alice-Miranda leaned forward eagerly.

The words whispered from his lips. "She died."

"Who died?" Alice-Miranda asked. "Not Miss Grimm, she's very much alive." She sat searching his face for answers. The tears were tracking down his lined cheeks, creating puddles in the dirt below. "Oh! Amelia," Alice-Miranda gasped, and clutched her hands to her mouth as though she had spoken a terrible word. "But how?"

Mr. Grump's chest heaved. "They said it was pneumonia. She hadn't even been sick—just a little cough. She went to bed and she never woke up."

"But people don't just die in their sleep." Alice-Miranda was shocked. "There must have been a reason."

"Ophelia rang me and said that Amelia had died. It was the worst moment of my life. She said that the doctor had been called and they tried to do everything possible but she had complications and there was nothing anyone could do." He paused. "But I didn't believe them. I didn't believe Ophelia and I told her it was her fault. I blamed her."

By now the poor man was sobbing quite uncontrollably. Alice-Miranda worried to see him in such a state.

"Mr. Grump, please calm down." She wrapped her arms around his shoulders. The shudders began to subside. "Surely you must have talked about things," she soothed.

"It was all a blur. There was a report and the funeral and lots of flowers and cards and people telling me how sorry they were. But Ophelia, I don't know. We didn't talk about it. I wrote her a note saying that I was going away. She sent her engagement ring back. I left my business, I left my home, and I've spent the past ten years walking around the world, trying to find someplace where I could forget." Mr. Grump pulled a box from his pocket and opened it. A diamond ring glinted in the sunlight.

"But you've never forgotten. That's her ring. Oh, poor Miss Grimm. It's no wonder she's so sad. You went walking all over the world and she locked herself away from it." Alice-Miranda stood up to stoke the fire and make another cup of tea.

"Somehow, after all these years, I ended up back here." Mr. Grump wiped away a tear.

"You've been in the school too, haven't you?" Alice-Miranda asked. "There was the blanket in the greenhouse and Mrs. Oliver's cakes—it was you?"

Aldous hung his head. "I wanted to know if Ophelia was still there, but when there was no sign, I gave up and came up here—to think," he said. "And then I saw you."

"Before, on the ledge, why did you call me Amelia?" Alice-Miranda asked.

"Because you, my dear girl, you are the image of my darling daughter," he replied.

Alice-Miranda handed him his mug and sat down. It certainly helped her to understand a few things.

"You must see her," said Alice-Miranda. There

was a sense of urgency in her voice that he found frightening.

"No, I couldn't. What I did to her was . . . unforgivable." He shook his head.

"Why are you here?" Alice-Miranda asked firmly.

"I don't know, really. I just needed to come back. I've spent all these years trying to forget and yet every night she comes to me in my dreams. I did a terrible thing. I was so afraid. How could I lose Evelyn and Amelia? What if I lost Ophelia too?"

"But you did lose Ophelia, Mr. Grump. And now you're back and you can find each other again. It's not too late. Miss Grimm's still young and you could get married and have your own family." Alice-Miranda's mind was racing ahead.

"I don't think she would ever want to see me again," said Mr. Grump as he wiped some crumbs from his beard.

"You've got nothing to lose, sir. You've come all this way." She stood up in front of him and placed her hands on his shoulders. "Do you love her?" Alice-Miranda looked deep into his eyes.

Slowly he nodded.

"Well, this calls for immediate action." Alice-Miranda ran toward her pack. "I'm going to do something I said that I absolutely would not," she declared. "No offense, Mr. Grump, but all these years you've been roaming the world have not been kind to your appearance. I have two more days out here and I plan to finish them. But that doesn't mean you can't get a head start. I'm going to call my father on the emergency phone, which I said would remain in my bottom drawer but which I'm *sure* Millie gave Mr. Charles to hide in the bottom of this backpack. Honestly, they all worry far too much." Alice-Miranda's words galloped out. "But you know, I do believe most firmly that all things happen for a reason. And the reason Millie gave Mr. Charles that phone was obviously because I was going to meet you. So I'm going to phone Daddy and he can send Cyril with Birdy straight away and you can go home to my house. Mummy will look after you and Daddy can give you some clean clothes and get you sorted out. When my hike is over you can come back to school and see Miss Grimm."

Mr. Grump looked at this amazing girl and was utterly speechless. There was no point arguing with her. Goodness, he didn't believe it possible that a child could be more determined than his own Amelia, but indeed this one was.

Alice-Miranda searched in the bottom of her backpack and found the phone. She called her father and spent the first five minutes explaining that she wasn't injured or lost or anything of the sort. Her father relayed the story to her mother, who was equally concerned. Cecelia said that she remembered there being a terrible tragedy at Winchesterfield-Downsfordvale quite some years before—and how dreadful for poor Mr. Grump and for dear Miss Grimm. They would send Cyril and Birdy right away.

Alice-Miranda said that she would meet Cyril in the large clearing on top of the mountain. This meant they had a way to walk yet, so she and Mr. Grump put out the fire, picked up their things and set off. She hoped that nobody would notice Birdy. She tried to remember where the girls would be and realized that they would likely be on the oval at sport. Maybe they wouldn't see him.

A short while later, as Cyril maneuvered Birdy toward the top of the mountain, Ophelia Grimm glanced out of her window. Her mind strayed to Alice-Miranda. She rather hoped that the child had given up and was waiting for Charlie to come and collect her. But for some reason she thought that rather unlikely.

Down on the sports field, Millie was startled to see Birdy overhead.

"Doesn't that helicopter belong to your little friend's parents?" Alethea asked, pointing up.

"I'm not sure," said Millie stoutly, but her heart

sank. She wondered if something terrible had happened and Alice-Miranda had found the phone smuggled into the bottom of her pack.

"So, poor little diddums can't cope out there in the big wide woods," Alethea smirked.

"Poor little diddums," the three marionettes chorused.

"Oh, shut up, you lot," Alethea roared.

Danika, Lizzy and Shelby had been getting on Alethea's nerves ever since she had caught them whining about their flat and dull hair after the mineral water washing. They were so ungrateful—she'd had her mother's hairdresser courier a special conditioner to her at school, and they hadn't even thanked her for it. She hadn't actually let them use any of it themselves, but she did let them wash her hair to see how well it worked.

Her puppets looked crushed. "Get over it!" Alethea growled. "You're not parrots."

Millie and the girls finished training and went back to the house. Perhaps she should call Alice-Miranda's mother to see if something was wrong.

"Hello, Mrs. Highton-Smith-Kennington-Jones, it's Millicent Jane McLoughlin-McTavish-McNoughton-McGill," Millie announced.

"Millicent, darling, how are you? Alice-Miranda has

told us all about you. Thank you for being such a kind friend to our girl. Please call me Cecelia."

"Mrs. High— Cecelia, I was wondering if there was a problem with Alice-Miranda on the hike?"

"No, darling, why ever would you think that?" Cecelia replied. Alice-Miranda had sworn her parents to secrecy about Cyril and Birdy collecting Mr. Grump. She prayed that nobody back at school had seen Birdy.

"Well, it's just that I thought I saw your helicopter this afternoon. It headed up onto the mountain and that's where Alice-Miranda would be by now, so I was just hoping there was nothing wrong." Millie's mind was racing. Surely Alice-Miranda hadn't been picked up. She was so reliable.

"No, Millie dear. I can't imagine why you would have thought it was Birdy. We haven't heard from Alice-Miranda at all," Cecelia fibbed. She desperately wanted to tell her the truth.

"Thanks, then. I must have been mistaken." Millie tried to sound convinced, as much for her own sake as Cecelia's. But the memory of the huge lettering on the helicopter's undercarriage—the initials H-S-K-J— was hard to ignore.

Chapter 38

The next two days dragged for Alice-Miranda. She was so excited about going home. She picked up all the flags and wrote in her diary. She investigated all sorts of places and drew pictures of animals she bumped into along the way. But really her mind was back at school. At first Alice-Miranda had no idea how to ensure that when Mr. Grump and Miss Grimm met again, Miss Grimm wouldn't be so upset that she'd hide in her office from him. But the one thing that being alone allowed Alice-Miranda to do was think. By midday on Friday, as she set off on the last couple of kilometers for home, she had a definite plan. But she needed lots of help.

Mummy and Daddy, Miss Higgins, Mrs. Smith and Mrs. Oliver, Mr. Charles, Miss Reedy and Mr. Plumpton, Jacinta, Millie and even Alethea. This had to be a team effort. If Miss Grimm was to rediscover the love of her life, then precision planning was required.

As she neared the far paddock gate, Alice-Miranda saw Mr. Charles waving furiously. Behind him it looked as though the whole school had come out to greet her. She began running toward them. There was a great shout of "Hooray!" as Alice-Miranda ran into Charlie's outstretched arms.

"Littl'un, you're back and you're safe!" He hugged her tightly.

Alice-Miranda looked around, expecting to see her friend. "Where's Millie?"

"I think she's in the library," Ivory replied.

Alice-Miranda began to worry. Why hadn't Millie come to meet her? She must have seen Birdy. What if she thought she'd abandoned the hike just like Alethea? Alice-Miranda needed to see her and let her know that she hadn't cheated.

The crowd of girls pushed in around her, shouting over the top of one another.

"Was it hard?"

"We've really missed you."

"Even Alethea said something about it not being the same without you."

Charlie lifted Alice-Miranda onto his shoulders and, surrounded by her friends, they returned in a triumphant parade to the quadrangle.

Miss Grimm was in the wardrobe watching.

"Oh, good grief. Don't tell me she did it?" she snapped. "What am I to do? That child will be the end of me."

Miss Higgins, Miss Reedy and all the other teachers were in the courtyard. They marveled at how well Alice-Miranda looked. She told them it was all because of Mrs. Oliver's amazing freeze-dried baked dinners. Mrs. Oliver beamed with pride.

While Alice-Miranda had been away, Mrs. Smith had decided to try a few new recipes and with Mrs. Oliver's help she had already perfected a chicken curry, Mongolian lamb hot pot and a few other more exotic dishes that had never before been seen at Winchesterfield-Downsfordvale. Although she'd tried to hide it, Miss Grimm had seemed especially impressed with the curry, which she hadn't had in years.

Alice-Miranda was tired. All she really wanted was a shower, a fresh set of clothes and a cup of tea. After answering loads of questions about however she had managed to do it, Alice-Miranda was led by Miss Higgins back to the dormitory to freshen up quickly. Mrs. Smith had cooked brownies in her honor, so she was wanted back in the dining room as soon as possible. The other girls had been told to wait for her.

"I'm so proud of you." Miss Higgins pushed a curl back from Alice-Miranda's face. "We're all proud of you." She smiled.

"Thank you, Miss Higgins," said Alice-Miranda. But she was concerned about something else. "I need to see Millie. I need to tell her that I didn't cheat."

"Of course you didn't cheat," said Miss Higgins, surprised. "Why would she think that?"

"It's a long story. Could I tell you after my shower?" asked Alice-Miranda, looking serious.

Suddenly there was a crackling sound in the air. Alice-Miranda jumped. Miss Higgins jumped too.

"Alice-Miranda Highton-Smith-Kennington-Jones, you are to report to the boatshed immediately," Miss Grimm's voice roared.

"What?" Alice-Miranda frowned. "What's she talking about?"

"I am talking about the regatta. The third of your challenges. You will compete against Alethea Goldsworthy this afternoon."

Miss Higgins looked around the room, wondering

how Miss Grimm had heard Alice-Miranda's question. She realized then that the technicians who had supposedly been fixing the security system must have been doing quite a bit more than that.

The girls and teachers in the dining room were equally stunned.

"But she doesn't have to race Alethea for another week," said Miss Reedy, puzzled. "Why ever has she brought the race forward? The poor child will be exhausted."

"Alethea Goldsworthy, you must also report to the boatshed immediately," Miss Grimm's voice boomed. "The race will commence at five p.m. and may I suggest, Miss Highton-Smith-Kennington-Jones, that you begin saying your farewells."

Millie had heard the announcement in the library. Alice-Miranda was her friend. She didn't deserve this. But what if she had cheated on the hike? Millie had seen the helicopter with her own eyes. What if Alice-Miranda was just as bad as Alethea? Millie was so confused. She wanted to support her friend, but she couldn't help wondering if it was all an act— Alice-Miranda's kindness, her sweetness, never saying a bad word about anyone?

Meanwhile, in the dining room, Miss Reedy raised herself to her feet.

"Quiet, girls. We must head to the lake immediately. I will ask Mrs. Oliver and Mrs. Smith if they can bring the tea. We must be there to support Alice-Miranda." She glared at Alethea.

"Why? Why would you support that little brat? She cheated on the hike, you know. Didn't you see the helicopter on Wednesday afternoon? She's nothing more than an upstart seven-and-a-quarter-year-old cheat!" Alethea screeched.

"What? Like you?" Danika stood up and glared at Alethea across the table. "You cheated last year, Alethea. You called your dear daddy and had him send the helicopter for you, then you spent the rest of the week at the Downsfordvale Manor Spa."

"Why, you lying—" Alethea reached across the table, as if she was about to strangle Danika. Shelby and Lizzy held her back.

The whole room erupted.

"I know someone who's definitely out of that group," Ashima said, and grinned.

"We're *all* out of the group," Lizzy called. "Come on, Shelby and Danika, let's go. We're sick of being told what to do. We're not your slaves, Alethea."

{235}

"I'm going to cheer for Alice-Miranda," said Shelby. She glared at Alethea, who was screaming like a madwoman.

"Girls, girls, be quiet," Miss Reedy yelled.

Miss Grimm was watching this outrageous scene from her wardrobe. "She cheated. The Head Prefect cheated. . . ." Ophelia's heart sank.

Chapter 39

"**M**iss Higgins, there is something important I need to tell you." Alice-Miranda and Miss Higgins were striding toward the lake.

"Yes, of course, what is it?" Miss Higgins was alarmed by the urgency in Alice-Miranda's voice.

"I know all about Miss Grimm," she began.

"What about Miss Grimm?" Miss Higgins's hands began to tremble. She stopped and faced Alice-Miranda.

"I know all about Amelia Grump and Aldous and the engagement and why Miss Grimm has a broken heart and why she has locked herself away in the study for all these years," Alice-Miranda blurted.

Miss Higgins gasped as though she had a bug caught in her throat.

"Don't be afraid. It's all going to be fine," Alice-Miranda continued.

"I'm not so sure. But we haven't got time for that now. It's nearly five p.m. and I can already see Alethea in her boat." Miss Higgins began to run toward the boatshed, with Alice-Miranda at her side.

Mr. Charles was by the water, with the *Emerald* tied up ready for Alice-Miranda to jump straight in. Just as she was about to push off, she noticed three adults walking toward the lake.

She turned to Miss Higgins. "There are Mummy and Daddy. And they've brought Mr. Grump too."

Miss Higgins felt faint. "Oh, this is going to be bad, very bad." She closed her eyes and said a silent prayer. "There's no time, sweetheart, you need to get out there."

Miss Higgins gave the *Emerald* a shove and the little boat glided out into the middle of the lake.

Alice-Miranda grabbed the rudder and ducked under the boom as the sail thudded across the boat. She caught up to Alethea just before the start line.

"I'm going to kill you," Alethea spat. "I hate you!"

Charlie had waited as long as he could to make

sure Alice-Miranda was almost level with Alethea. He raised the starter gun into the air and fired. The girls were to sail around the island three times.

Miss Grimm was watching the race through the closed-circuit television camera mounted on the boatshed. Alice-Miranda was gaining on Alethea, but Ophelia was confident that the brat wouldn't be able to beat her. Alethea's new skiff had cost thousands and apparently a donkey could have sailed her and won.

"Go, darling!" Cecelia Highton-Smith shouted from the bank as the boats rounded the island for their first pass. Alice-Miranda was behind and Alethea seemed to be pulling away.

"Come on, Alice-Miranda, use the wind, use the wind," her father called.

The whole school was cheering loudly. Mrs. Smith and Mrs. Oliver had forgotten all about the tea and were jumping up and down as if on pogo sticks.

"Come on, my girl, you can do it!" Mrs. Oliver shouted.

"Beat that brat!" Mrs. Smith screamed over the top.

Alethea was almost five lengths in front as they completed the first lap.

In the meantime, Millie had been unable to concentrate in the library. She ran out of the building and down to the water's edge. She immediately recognized Alice-Miranda's mother from her photograph.

"Hello, Mrs. High— Cecelia, I'm Millie." She smiled.

"Hello, Millie, this is my husband, Hugh, and this is a friend, Aldous. Alice-Miranda met him in the mountains on Wednesday and I rather think she rescued him," said Cecelia.

"So she didn't get picked up?" Millie frowned.

"No, of course not. Birdy and Cyril came for Mr. Grump. I wanted to tell you but Alice-Miranda had sworn me to secrecy. She wanted to explain it all herself." Cecelia smiled.

Millie felt a surge of relief. Alice-Miranda wasn't a cheat. She was her wonderful best friend. She ran to the water's edge just as the *Emerald* passed.

"Go, Alice-Miranda, go!" she shouted over the top of everyone.

Alice-Miranda looked over and saw Millie waving and cheering. She felt so relieved—her mother must have explained everything. She turned her focus back to the race.

She was catching up with Alethea. As they were about to finish the second lap, Alice-Miranda was only a couple of lengths behind. Alethea's boat seemed to be lying lower in the water and the *Emerald* was gaining all the time. A gust of wind propelled Alice-

Miranda forward and she was almost level. Then Alethea reached backward and hit a switch on the stern of her skiff. Suddenly it took off at a ridiculous pace.

"She's got a motor," Danika shouted, pointing at the froth behind Alethea's boat.

"She's cheating again," Lizzy called.

Alice-Miranda was now half a lap behind. Her heart began to sink. She didn't want to have to leave Winchesterfield-Downsfordvale. She belonged here.

"Go, darling, go!" her father urged. "Use the wind."

A huge gust propelled her forward again and she began to make up some ground. Alethea's boat really did look to be sinking. Alethea must have realized it too, because she started bailing the water with her hands.

"Look!" Millie shouted as the boats came back into view. "The *Emerald*'s just nosed ahead."

The spectators shouted in chorus, "Go, Alice-Miranda, go!"

The finish line was only meters away. Alice-Miranda was ahead. Alethea was up to her waist in water but somehow her boat was still moving forward. Just as the girls were about to cross the line, Alice-Miranda surged ahead and Alethea's boat sank like a brick.

The crowd erupted. Alice-Miranda looked behind her to see a waterlogged Alethea clinging to the mast of her skiff.

"Alethea," she cried. "Swim over here."

Alethea was crying ferociously. "No, go away. I hate you!" she screamed.

Charlie was already motoring toward Alethea in the dinghy.

"Well done," he called to Alice-Miranda. "Don't worry. I'll get her." He sped toward the crumpled mess in the middle of the lake.

Alice-Miranda sailed to the jetty, where her father lifted her out of the *Emerald* and onto the shore. Everyone was cheering and clapping. Her mother hugged her, then Mr. Grump did, and then a long line of girls and teachers took their turns congratulating her.

Chapter 40

The celebrations seemed to last for ages. Alice-Miranda had done it. She had earned her place at Winchesterfield-Downsfordvale. Everyone had seen her do it. The test results were a formality.

Ophelia Grimm had watched as the events unfolded. Alice-Miranda had won the regatta fair and square; she'd conquered the hike and passed the test with flying colors. On the other hand, Alethea—the child she had put so much faith in—was nothing but a cheat. Sitting in her wardrobe watching the contest, Ophelia realized that her life was a lie. She was a fraud—here she was in charge of a school, a magnificent school with wonderful children, and yet she had shut herself away from it all. Her judgment of people had been clouded for so many years. She had forgotten to do what she should always have done: trust her instincts. Ophelia stood up, straightened her skirt, put on her blazer and strode out of the study and into the afternoon sunshine.

"Look!" Millie pointed at the figure walking toward the lake. An eerie glow surrounded the woman as the sun shone behind her. "Is that . . . Is it Miss Grimm?" Millie shouted.

The whole school gasped as they caught sight of Ophelia. The girls buzzed:

"What's she doing?"

"Why is she here?"

"She can't make you leave."

Miss Grimm strode toward the crowd with her head held high. Not a word was spoken as she reached them.

"I am not here to expel you, Alice-Miranda," said Miss Grimm. "I am here to congratulate you. Your test results." She held up the paper with *97%* emblazoned in the top right-hand corner. "I know when I am defeated. You have secured your place here and I will not . . . I will not set you any further ridiculous challenges. I have been a very sad and bitter woman these past ten years. I wonder if perhaps you could consider forgiving me." Miss Grimm stared at the surprising child.

"Oh, Miss Grimm, of course I forgive you." Alice-Miranda ran forward and wrapped her arms around Miss Grimm's middle. There was another collective gasp from the school. Miss Grimm didn't seem to know what to do. Her eyes welled and suddenly she did what any self-respecting grown-up would do. She hugged Alice-Miranda right back.

"I have someone here who wants to see you," said Alice-Miranda, pulling away. She motioned to Mr. Grump, who was standing behind her father. Miss Grimm looked up.

"Oh!" It was Miss Grimm's turn to gasp. Tears flooded her eyes. "Is it really you?" She swallowed. The temptation to turn and run back to the safety of her study was almost too much. But for some reason her legs were frozen to the spot.

"Ophelia." Mr. Grump strode forward. "Ophelia, I am so sorry. I ruined everything. I've spent so many years trying to forget. But I could never forget you. Can you ever forgive me?" Aldous hung his head.

The whole school seemed to have something caught in their throats. Tears fell like waterfalls.

"Aldous, how? I thought you were . . ."

"I can explain everything—if you will just give me

another chance. I know I don't deserve it, but I—I love you."

"And I love you too." Ophelia fell into his arms and he peppered her face with kisses.

At long last Jacinta broke the silence. "Three cheers for Miss Grimm. Hip, hip, hooray! Hip, hip, hooray! Hip, hip, hooray! And three cheers for Alice-Miranda. Hip, hip, hooray! Hip, hip, hooray! Hip, hip, hooray!"

As the sun set that evening, for the first time in a long time Winchesterfield-Downsfordvale truly felt like the happiest school on earth. . . .

And just in case you're wondering...

Miss Grimm and Mr. Grump were married within a month in the chapel at Winchesterfield-Downsfordvale. Miss Grimm had a beautiful bouquet of hollyhocks and daffodils, jonquils and irises. Every one of the girls, staff and the parents said it was the best party they had ever been to. Ophelia thought about a hyphenated surname but decided to stick with Grimm.

Miss Higgins was married three weeks later to Constable Derby. She's back at work because Miss Grimm said that she simply couldn't live without her.

Jacinta Headlington-Bear won the national gymnastics championships for her age group.

Mr. Charles won the local garden competition and was particularly complimented on his flowerbeds.

Mrs. Oliver perfected her formula for FDF—Freeze-dried Foods—and is in the process of establishing an organization to feed the starving people of the world. Mrs. Smith spent two weeks of her holidays helping Dolly in the laboratory and the other time with her grandchildren in America.

Alethea Goldsworthy left Winchesterfield-Downsfordvale in rather a rush. She is currently enrolled at Sainsbury Palace School, where there is a very large new library under construction.

And if you're wondering about the new Head Prefect . . . Well, Miss Grimm decided to break with tradition and offer it to Alice-Miranda. But Alice-Miranda refused to accept, saying that Danika would do a much better job. After all, she had plenty of time. She was still only seven and one-quarter.

Cast of characters

THE HIGHTON-SMITH-KENNINGTON-JONES HOUSEHOLD

Alice-Miranda Highton-Smith-Kennington-Jones	Only child, seven and one-quarter years of age
Cecelia Highton-Smith	Alice-Miranda's doting mother
Hugh Kennington-Jones	Alice-Miranda's doting father
Dolly Oliver	Family cook, part-time food technology scientist
Cyril	Helicopter pilot
Mr. Greening	Gardener
Birdy	Bell Jet Ranger helicopter

WINCHESTERFIELD-DOWNSFORDVALE ACADEMY
FOR PROPER YOUNG LADIES STAFF

Miss Ophelia Grimm	Headmistress
Miss Louella Higgins	Personal secretary to the headmistress
Miss Livinia Reedy	English teacher
Mr. Josiah Plumpton	Science teacher
Mr. Cornelius Trout	Music teacher
Miss Benitha Wall	Sports teacher
Cook (Mrs. Doreen Smith)	Cook
Charlie Weatherly (Mr. Charles)	Gardener
Howie (Mrs. Howard)	House mistress
Shaker	Another house mistress

STUDENTS

Millicent Jane McLoughlin-McTavish-McNoughton-McGill	Best friend and roommate
Madeline Bloom	Friend
Ivory Hicks	Friend
Ashima Divall	Friend
Susannah Dare	Friend

Jacinta Headlington-Bear	Talented gymnast, school's second-best tantrum thrower and, surprisingly, a friend
Alethea Goldsworthy	Head Prefect, school's very best tantrum thrower and enemy of most girls
Danika	Alethea's friend
Lizzy	Alethea's friend
Shelby	Alethea's friend

OTHER

Miss Critchley	Teacher at Ellery Prep
Ambrose McLoughlin-McTavish	Millie's grandfather
Addison Goldsworthy	Alethea's father
Harold	Addison Goldsworthy's butler and chauffeur

Nana Jones's Apple Pie

(THE BEST APPLE PIE EVER!)

Ask an adult to help you.

INGREDIENTS

Apple filling

4–6 large Granny Smith apples

Tiny amount of water to cover the bottom of the saucepan

3–4 cloves

2 tablespoons of sugar

Pastry

4½ tablespoons of butter

5 tablespoons of milk

2 cups of self-rising flour

Extra milk and sugar for brushing on top

METHOD
Apple filling
- Preheat oven to 375° F
- Peel and slice the apples carefully—you don't want any apple skin in the pie (it's just not nice)
- Place the sliced apples, water, cloves and sugar in a saucepan
- Bring to the boil and simmer for 10 minutes or until tender

Pastry
- Melt the butter and milk together over low heat
- Add enough flour to make a stiff dough—this can be a little tricky
- Divide the mixture in half and roll out both sections separately on greaseproof paper to make the top and bottom of the piecrust
- Place one piece of pastry into a pie plate—make sure that it comes up the sides
- Spoon the apple mixture into the pie plate (take out the cloves first—they taste really yucky if you leave them in and accidentally eat one—believe me!)
- Place the other piece of pastry on top to make a lid. Make sure that it fits well—I like to get my fingers in and press it down around the edges
- Use the leftover pastry to make a crisscross pattern

with little balls on the top. Be creative—this is a really fun bit!

- Brush a small amount of milk on the lid and sprinkle some sugar over the top (just a little bit)
- Bake the pie for 20–25 minutes
- Serve hot with ice cream or cream (or both!)
- Eat and enjoy!

Acknowledgments

I have been a teacher for such a big part of my life, and Alice-Miranda is so many children I have adored. Children who have made me laugh and cry and who have continually surprised and inspired me with their determination, their humility, their generosity and their humor.

Alice-Miranda and I couldn't have made this journey alone—there are many people who have supported and encouraged me along the way. And so to them I say thank you.

My most ardent supporter, my husband, Ian, has been known to laugh, particularly when I am pulling faces trying to imagine what something looks like in words, but he never tires of listening and reading—

and in the process very often comes up with wonderful ideas to add to the story. He is the reason I am able to do what I do, because above all else he believes in me—even when I don't. He knows I think he's amazing—and now everyone else who's read this does too!

Thank you to Nerrilee Weir, clearly the cleverest rights manager in Australia, and to Catherine Drayton at Inkwell Management, for helping Alice-Miranda get her passport to the United States (and beyond!).

To my dear friend Sandy Campbell, who, in the midst of her epic battle, sat up all night and read *Alice-Miranda*. It was Sandy who wrote an e-mail to my publisher recommending the story. Although Sandy is not here to see Alice-Miranda on her journey, I feel she is certainly with us in spirit, with the warmest of hugs and yummiest of scones, cheering us on. I miss her very much.

To my mother, Jennifer, and my beloved grandmothers, Betty Earnell and Edna Jones (the real Nana Jones), thank you for passing on your wonderful recipes and teaching me how to cook.

To my sisters and brother-in-law, Sarah, Natalie and Trent, thank you for listening to all my harebrained ideas and reading manuscripts in record time. And to Darcy and Flynn, well, thank you for being you—you inspire me and I love you both to bits!

To my Poppy and Grandad, Norman and Colin; my dad, Gary; my stepdaughter, Olivia; and my mother- and father-in-law, John and Joan—the best cheer squad I could have hoped for. I know John would be very proud to see Alice-Miranda making her way in the world.

And lastly a huge thank-you to the staff, students and parents at Abbotsleigh, who have given me loads of encouragement and support. It is a joy to share stories with the girls, and I love that they are so honest in telling me what they really think, especially when a response is prefaced with, "Well, you know, Mrs. Harvey, I really like you, it's just that . . ."

About
the Author

Jacqueline Harvey has spent her working life teaching in girls' boarding schools. She is pleased to say that she has never yet encountered a headmistress like Miss Grimm, but she has come across quite a few girls who remind her a little of Alice-Miranda.

Jacqueline has published three novels for young readers in her native Australia. Her first picture book, *The Sound of the Sea*, was named a Children's Book Council of Australia Honor Book. She is currently working on Alice-Miranda's next adventure.

COMING SOON
Alice-Miranda's next adventure—

Alice-Miranda on Holiday

Here's a sneak peek:

Alice-Miranda Highton-Smith-Kennington-Jones said goodbye to her friends on the steps of Winchesterfield Manor.

"Please try to be brave, Mrs. Smith." She wrapped her arms around the cook's waist.

"Dear girl." Mrs. Smith sniffled into her tissue, then fished around in her apron pocket to retrieve a small parcel wrapped in greaseproof paper. "Some brownies for the drive."

"Oh, Mrs. Smith, my favorites! You really are the best brownie cook in the whole world. I'll share them with Mummy and Jacinta. You know, I was thinking you should make them for Kennington's. I'm sure we'd sell kazillions. Imagine: 'Mrs. Smith's Scrumptious Melt-in-Your-Mouth Chocolate Brownies.'" Alice-Miranda underlined the invisible words in the air. "Wouldn't that be amazing—you'd be famous!"

Mrs. Smith turned the color of beetroot and shook her head. "Off you go," she said, and smiled. "And please tell Dolly I'm looking forward to seeing her next week."

Alice-Miranda stepped back and moved along the line.

"Now, you look after those flowers while I'm gone, Mr. Charles," she said, smiling up at her weathered friend. His eyes, the color of cornflowers, sparkled in the morning sunlight and he brushed a work-worn hand across the corner of his face.

"Ah, lass, I'll have those blooms perfect by the time you get back," he said with a nod.

Alice-Miranda stepped closer, wrapping her arms around his middle.

"Off with you now," he said, and patted her shoulder.

Mr. Plumpton and Miss Reedy stood side by side. His nose glowed red, while she maintained her usual dignified stance.

"Thank you, Miss Reedy." Alice-Miranda offered

her tiny hand, which Livinia Reedy shook most vigorously. "I've had a wonderful term."

"You have a lovely break, Alice-Miranda. It's hard to believe you've been here only three months." Miss Reedy smiled down at her youngest student. The girl was a constant source of amazement.

"And Mr. Plumpton, your science lessons have been truly fantastic. I will never in my life forget that volcano experiment. All that frothing and fizzing and then—*boom!*" Alice-Miranda laughed.

Mr. Plumpton's forehead wrinkled. "That wasn't my best work, Alice-Miranda. Not quite the outcome I was expecting." He blushed deeply from his shirt collar to the tip of his very bald head.

"But Mr. Plumpton, it was magnificent—even if it did blow rather a large hole in the ceiling and spew that icky liquid all over the lab."

"Yes, well, I can only imagine how the volcano's vent ended up with a cork wedged in it." He tried not to, but couldn't help showing an embarrassed smirk.

Next in line stood Mrs. Derby. Alice-Miranda was only just getting used to Miss Higgins's new name.

"You have a lovely holiday, sweetheart," the young woman said, beaming.

"Thank you, Miss Higgins, I mean, Mrs. Derby," Alice-Miranda corrected herself.

Mrs. Derby knelt down and brushed a stray curl behind Alice-Miranda's ear. The tiny child leaned forward and threw her arms around Mrs. Derby's neck.

"Now, what was that for?" she asked, as surprised as she had been the first time Alice-Miranda had offered such affection.

"Just because I love you," the tiny girl whispered.

At the end of the line loomed the headmistress, Miss Grimm, in a striking magenta suit. Her hair, now swept up loosely, no longer pinned her face into a pinched scowl. Today she was elegant and quite beautiful.

"Alice-Miranda," she barked sternly, and then, as if remembering she was no longer *that* person, she cleared her throat and began again.

"Alice-Miranda." This time her tone was soft. "Thank you for your hard work this term. It has been a pleasure." Her dark eyes smiled and her mouth curved upward.

"No, thank *you,* Miss Grimm. Winchesterfield-Downsfordvale Academy for Proper Young Ladies really is the most beautiful school in the whole wide world and you are the best headmistress in the world too. Even when you were, well, upset and angry pretty much all of the time, I knew that wasn't really you. You were far too stylish and lovely to be as mean as all that." Alice-Miranda stopped suddenly.

Miss Grimm's eyes narrowed.

"What I meant to say, Miss Grimm, is that I knew it wasn't the real you; the one who spied on us and never came out to see the girls and the staff and wouldn't let Mrs. Smith take holidays or Mr. Charles plant flowers, or Jacinta go to the gymnastics championships—"

"Stop!" Miss Grimm held up her hand.

"But Miss Grimm, what I really meant to say—"

"Enough," Miss Grimm cut her off again, her steely eyes threatening. "No more. Do not say another word, Alice-Miranda."

Suddenly Ophelia's face crumpled and she found herself smiling at this infernal child with her cascading chocolate curls. She bent down to meet Alice-Miranda's brown-eyed gaze.

"Now, Miss Highton-Smith-Kennington-Jones, as your headmistress I am commanding that during this term break you must assure me that you will under no circumstances spend time studying for ridiculous academic tests, nor will you set off on any wilderness walks on your own and you most *definitely* will not train for onerous physical challenges. After what I put you through at the beginning of the term, I expect nothing less than three weeks of purely childish pursuits befitting that of a girl aged seven and one-quarter."

"Oh dear, I am sorry, Miss Grimm, but I can't guarantee any of those things," Alice-Miranda whispered.

"And why ever not, young lady?" Miss Grimm snapped.

"Because, Miss Grimm, I'm actually now seven and a half." Alice-Miranda beamed.

Before she knew what she was doing, Ophelia Grimm leaned forward and hugged Alice-Miranda tightly.

"Thank you, Miss Grimm." Alice-Miranda hugged her right back. "And you and Mr. Grump enjoy your honeymoon, too. Goodness knows you've waited long enough for it."

Now it was Ophelia's turn to blush.

Alice-Miranda ran toward her mother's shiny silver car parked at the bottom of the steps.

"Come on, darling, time to go home," said Cecelia Highton-Smith, dabbing a tissue to her eyes.

"Hurry up, Alice-Miranda," Jacinta called from the backseat. "Bye, everyone," she shouted, waving furiously.

The staff could hardly believe just how much things

had changed in the eleven weeks Alice-Miranda had been at Winchesterfield-Downsfordvale. And who would have thought that Jacinta Headlington-Bear—the school's former second-best tantrum thrower—would ever be invited home for term break?

Excerpt copyright © 2010 by Jacqueline Harvey. Published in the United States by Delacorte Press, an imprint of Random House Children's Books, a division of Random House, Inc., New York. Originally published in paperback by Random House Australia, Sydney, in 2010.